Rennell Rodd

Ballads of the Fleet

And other Poems

Rennell Rodd

Ballads of the Fleet
And other Poems

ISBN/EAN: 9783744787307

Printed in Europe, USA, Canada, Australia, Japan

Cover: Foto ©Andreas Hilbeck / pixelio.de

More available books at **www.hansebooks.com**

FRANCIS DRAKE

BALLADS OF THE FLEET

AND OTHER POEMS

BY

RENNELL RODD

AUTHOR OF 'THE VIOLET CROWN,' ETC.

WITH A PHOTOGRAVURE FRONTISPIECE

EDWARD ARNOLD

LONDON AND NEW YORK

1897

TO

MY MANY FRIENDS

IN THE FINEST SERVICE IN THE WORLD

WHO PROUDLY HOLD UNQUESTIONED

THE INHERITANCE OF DRAKE

PREFACE

THE first five poems in the present volume, together with a Ballad of the Armada, which, though later in historical sequence, was published in an earlier collection, are a partial realisation of a projected series of ballads on the great Elizabethan mariners which it has long been my ambition to write. But other calls and occupations have left but little time available to be devoted to a subject which well deserves to claim our undivided attention.

In dealing with the following episodes in the life of Sir Francis Drake, which have been the leisure occupation of several Egyptian summers, I have for the most part, without neglecting to consult original sources, followed the excellent narrative of my friend Mr. Julian

Corbett, who has himself approached in the spirit of a poet the romantic story of the great adventurer.   He appears to me to have grasped in a masterly manner the true meaning and importance of the much-debated trial and death of Doughty, and in subscribing to his conclusions it is satisfactory that one's predilections should without any violence coincide with one's sense of justice.

In the Appendix to the Hakluyt Society's edition of *The World Encompassed*, certain documents are published, purporting to be first-hand evidence, which attribute to the character and conduct of Drake a very' different colour from that which popular sentiment and tradition have handed down.   But Drake, like all men who have rapidly conquered popularity and success, had no lack of enemies, and we may well afford to assume that these documents are the work of detractors and malcontents who had their own reasons for seeking to blacken the great sea-captain's name, even if we do not trace them to the immediate inspiration of John Doughty, the brother of

Thomas, of whom he had of course made an irreconcilable enemy. Drake had, we learn elsewhere, at a critical moment had occasion to stigmatise Francis Fletcher as "the falsest knave alive."

In forming an estimate of Drake's conduct on this occasion, there are three points which appear to me conclusive. In the first place, the charges which have been brought against him are wholly alien to the nature of the man as we know him from other sources; secondly, his conduct was never called in question upon his return home, though his opponents in the Council were many and influential; and in the third place, John Doughty, whom he had spared, though he believed him implicated in his brother's treachery, was subsequently a fellow-conspirator with a Spanish agent in a plot against his life.

Therefore, in spite of any documents which recent research has brought to light, we may be content to abide by the verdict of the men of his own time and the reasonable judgment of Dr. Johnson.

The other poems included in the present series will, I trust, tell their own story and require no further introduction ; one only of them, the Ballad of Richard Peake, has been previously published, in the *English Illustrated Magazine.*

R. R.

CAIRO, *September* 1897.

CONTENTS

CHILDREN OF THE SEA

BALLADS OF THE FLEET

CHILDREN OF THE SEA

In the Medway mouth by Chatham the King's ships
    lay at ease,
The fleet that Tudor Henry built, who was lord of
    the narrow seas ;—

Across the bay were the shipwrights' yards where they
    laid the sturdy keel,
And there day through rang hammer stroke, and
    hissed the strident steel ;

And there they bent the good ship's ribs, and
    trimmed the taper tree,
To lift the wide wings windward that bear men over
    the sea ;

The old dismasted war-hulks, whose travelling days
    were done,
Lay moored in the quiet reaches where they blistered
    in the sun.

And many a shore-bird there had found a cranny for
    its nest,
And children's faces thronged the ports of those old
    barks at rest.

In such an ark of olden days, moored hard by
    Chatham dock,
There was lodged a sturdy man of God, one Drake
    of Tavistock :

A stern, unyielding Western man, who held with the
    stern new creed,
And deemed that the word was lifeless which did not
    prompt the deed ;

The creed that yet had its evil days of blood and of
    fire to face
Before the faith was 'stablished that has formed the
    English race.

He had seen his homestead burning long since, and
 fled for life
Across the Dartmoor highlands with his new-born
 child and wife;

What time the Western counties rose, that famous
 Whitsuntide,
When stalwart Reformation men were on the losing
 side.

But now was peace in all the land through Edward's
 ebbing days,
Before the torch Queen Mary lit had set the shires
 ablaze;

And here of a Sunday morning, in sunshine, rain, or
 sleet,
The rough sea-folk would gather to the chaplain of
 the Fleet:

For they that go abroad in ships are earnest men at
 prayer,
And they prayed as they would in their own plain way,
 and as yet none vexed them there.

So half a score of sturdy lads grew up between the
    decks,
And paddled in the ebbing shoals, and played at raids
    and wrecks—

Their small black boats would bear them over the
    reaches wide,
Where the mimic billows tossed their manes when
    the home-wind met the tide,

With quick young hands for tiller and sheet alert to
    the pulse of the breeze,
And frank young fearless laughter tuned to the
    tumbled seas ;

While the mother would watch with anxious eyes
    from the deck of their floating home
The track where the children guided a nutshell craft
    in the foam.

They were nursed on the cradling water by fostering
    wind and wave,
And as they had lived, so in after years in the sea
    they found their grave.

There, half in wonder and half in awe, they had heard
grave men debate
Dark rumours of the death of kings, and tidings big
with fate ;

And they saw the Kentish yeomen arm, and march
with pike and sword,
When Wyatt mustered round his flag the servants of
the Lord ;—

They heard of the battles lost and won, and the good
blood spilt in vain,
And the infant lips were taught to curse the league
with Rome and Spain.

So years rolled on, and the eldest-born went forth and
took his chance,
A 'prentice hand on a ketch that plied to the Channel
ports and France.

Dark days had set on England, dark days for such as
Drake,
And lurid through the darkness shone the fagot and
the stake ;—

It was little enough like boyhood's dream, a dreary life
    at the best,
With danger and toil for shipmates, and hunger oft as
    a guest;

It was little enough like boyhood's dream—when the
    light on a sunset sail,
To eyes that followed the outward bound, was more
    than a fairy tale;

To crouch chilled through on the dripping planks,
    and watch for the roving lights,
When green seas break on the dipping prow through
    the endless wintry nights,

When the blast drives down from Bergen, and the
    cloud-banks blot the moon,
And the evil sea is a churning race from the chalk
    cliffs to the dune;

But the mariner's boy was taught his craft, and in
    service learned to rule,
And he braced his nerve and he trained his eye in a
    hard and thankless school.

He saw the lilied flag of Guise at Calais oust his
　　Queen's,
And the fleet of England sail with Spain to battle at
　　Gravelines ;

And in the ports of Maas and Scheldt they found no
　　better cheer,
There too the shadow of the cowl fell deeper year by
　　year :—

For a great unrest had touched the time, the world's
　　deep heart was stirred,
There rang across the northern blasts a voice that
　　would be heard,

A voice that shook the ocean shores where freedom
　　wills to dwell,
From Zealand and the English cliffs to Nantes and
　　La Rochelle :

The night of years broke into dawn, and now in a
　　broader day
Men's conscience craved for warrant from those who
　　bade obey ;

And lest this dire contagion spread, and free thought
    breathe again,
The flag of the Holy Office waved over the ports of
    Spain ;

And through the Flemish sand-hills and up the
    Holland dykes
The hounds of God were on the trail to flesh the
    Spanish pikes.

But where their withering mandate fell deep slumbering
    passions woke,
For simple men grew great of heart and turned against
    their yoke,

And the deed of high endeavour was no more to the
    favoured few,
But brain and heart were the measure of what every
    man might do.

The wronged took arms and sought redress at their
    own risk and fee,
Shook off their feet the bloody dust, and gathered in
    the sea ;

The London merchants mounted guns, and armed the
    trading barque,
The boatmen left their nets and lines to follow de la
    Mark,

So corsairs swept the narrow seas, and watched the
    highway south,
While justice in her ruder form spoke through the
    cannon's mouth ;

Long years the trembling nations paused, the red fires
    smouldered low,
While monarchs knew within their gates the inter-
    necine foe ;

Till there arose in island England a Queen, by God's
    own grace,
Who gathered in her ample heart the heart of all her
    race,

The race which loving freedom of their own free will
    obeyed,
Till champions mustered round her, and trust with
    trust repaid ;

She saw the crisis of the age, absorbed her nation's
    faith,
And faced a world's defiance with battle to the death.

Through those dark years of doubt and stress the
    coaster plied her trade,
The preacher's lad grew great and strong, and so the
    man was made.

Such was the school of Francis Drake, who sowed in
    the years to be
The seed of England's empire in the furrows of the
    sea !

SAN JUAN DE LUA

SAN JUAN DE LUA

THIS is a tale of a treason, with the fate of a world in
    its wake—
The treason of Don Alvarez and the oath of Francis
    Drake !

It was nigh twelve months since Captain John had
    beat out of Plymouth Sound
With the Queen's tall ships the *Jesus* and the *Minion*
    southward bound ;

And Drake in the little *Judith* had sailed in his
    kinsman's train,
With his all on earth in the venture to trade in the
    Spanish Main.

They met with a gale in Biscay, they had started late
     in the year,
And the Queen's tall ship the *Jesus* was leaky and ill
     to steer;

So they halted in Grand Canary and righted their
     disarray,
Recaulked the straining timbers and then to the
     South away!

They harried the Lisbon traders with Fenner's name
     for a plea,
For the law of quick reprisals was the grim old law at
     sea;

And the *Grace of God* got an English name and an
     English flag at the main
Ere they sailed for Margarita and the ocean world of
     Spain.

There's many a tale were well forgot,—there's little
     enough to boast
Of the work they did those winter months in the
     bights of the Guinea coast.

They did not barter their English gold for the palm-
oil or the date,

But the hulls that came in ballast went out with a
living freight ;

On an evil day, John Hawkins, you took up with an
evil trade,

And you set your course by a luckless star with the
fruit of a bloody raid !

Though many had held it was God's work too, while
in that dark Afric hell

Before the inhuman altars the weak and the captive
fell ;

While the wretch foredoomed to the slaughter might
live to be sold a slave,

The brand be plucked from the burning and a soul
be won to save.

But little recked they of doubts or fears that vexed
the soul of the wise,

They did as the world did round them, and they
claimed their share of the prize ;

And their sons shall make atonement, in the years
    that are to be,
For the freight they bore to the New World's shore
    through the still Sargasso Sea.

———

They were seven weeks in the ocean and never a
    a sail went by,
Cramped in the lonely vastness of infinite sea and
    sky :

But ever the stars moved eastward, and the new stars
    rose to ken,
The awe of the waters scared them, and they longed
    for the paths of men :

Till at last with the sunrise glimmer there rose through
    an opal sea
A shadowy range of islands and the haze of a land on
    the lee ;

And the mariner's boy stared wondering eyed,—for
    the wings of the wind were furled,
And the capes hung high in the still mirage of dawn
    on a phantom world ;

A land where never our island oaks had fared since
    the years began,
Until John Hawkins taught them the path of the
    Englishman.

Then a breeze came perfume-laden from the heart of
    the tropic zone,
And crinkling waves tossed round them the drift of a
    shore unknown :

And the winged fish rose on the face of the deep to
    skim like a cloud of spray
From edge to edge of the curling blue and into the
    blue away ;

But the sun still beckoned them westward till he
    sank in a blaze of fire
On the fabled hills of a thousand dreams and the
    goal of a world's desire ;

While the parting mists wreathed upwards in delicate
    rosy whirls,
And there peered through a rift in the broken veil
    the peaks of the isle of pearls.

Now Philip in his great wisdom had laid England
    under a ban,
And never a New World settler might trade with an
    Englishman.

But the lust of the land was on them, the craving of
    men confined
For a draft of the fresh spring water, the snuff of the
    off-shore wind,

So they landed in Margarita in despite of the King of
    Spain,
They paid their footing in honest gold and quickened
    their hearts again.

And they saw the New World's mountains rise up
    from a palm-fringed shore
Where ever on fangs of coral the long surf-rollers
    roar ;

Those crags that Amyas Preston and Somers are soon
    to scale
By pathways hewn through the tangled brakes in the
    blinding mists and hail,

Up mountain walls impregnable to be conquered
    stair by stair
Till Sant Iago fall a prey to the men who grandly
    dare.

But they skirted steep La Guayra till they came to a
    lonely bay,
In the gulf that men called " Triste," where was none
    to say them nay ;

And there they abode careening, refitting the masts
    and spars,
And they learned the signs of the seasons and the
    march of the tropic stars.

Here all was a land of marvel, the fireflies' glimmer
    at night,
The shore where the sea-weed gardens rock under the
    phosphor light ;

The great tree-ferns and the coco palms, and the
    wild lime's sweet perfume,
The edge of the forest crimsoned with the great
    hibiscus bloom,

Where clinging from each green tangle hang down
    like a cluster of bells
Purple and pink and scarlet the frail convolvulus
    cells ;

Where the moth-birds pause and flutter a shower of
    gems in the air,
Dip slender bills in the waxen cups and drink of the
    nectar there.

So a passion of high adventure came over that English
    crew,—
They had seen the New World's promise and the way
    that the east wind blew,

They had only stood on the threshold, on the marge
    of the siren west,
But the magic wand had touched them, and now they
    would never rest.

From thence they began their trading—the peace of
    the realms their plea,
And the right of open harbour to all from the open
    sea.

The Spanish governors shook their heads, but they
    made protest in vain,
And the Guinea freight was bartered in despite of the
    King of Spain ;

For the settlers made them welcome, and came off in
    the night aboard,
Or they claimed their rights of market at the point of
    the naked sword ;

And it prospered those free-traders till deep in the
    Jesus' hold
Was a smouldering fire of jewels and a shimmer of
    virgin gold.

Then merry at heart they hoisted sail with a home-
    ward facing prow,
For each had a share in the venture, and each was a
    rich man now.

It was northward first, then eastward, the course that
    the Gulf Stream ran,
Where it swept to the bend of Cuba from the elbow
    of Yucatan ;

And there the storms broke on them, and the wave
    came nigh to whelm :
The hulls were foul, and they made no way, and the
    Jesus lost her helm:

Oh nerve of iron and heart of oak were set in the
    simple mould
Of the men who sped to the unknown seas in the
    crazy craft of old !

They drove past misty headlands with the chill of
    death on their souls,
And they heard the thunders breaking over uncharted
    shoals ;

And thrice each deemed that the rest were lost, and
    scoured the seas in vain,
And thrice each fought in a week of storm with the
    might of the hurricane ;

They saw no sun in the daytime, and the stars at
    night were blind,
And they sped for a week on an unknown course at
    the mercy of the wind ;

Till their desperate hearts were broken, and as men
  who have nought to lose,
They ran right in to the hornet's nest in the port of
  Vera Cruz.

So they moored in the outer harbour, while the ships'
  bells rang to prayer,
And they cried on the Lord who had spared their
  lives to be with them even there ;

For this was the way with the western folk in storm
  or battle or raid,
They wrought with a will, and they fought with a will,
  and so with a will they prayed.

For strong they said are the whirlwinds, and long is
  the arm of the foe,
But the finger of God is stronger in the path where
  seamen go.

Now it chanced that there in the haven the Indies'
  Plate Fleet lay,
To wait for the convoy galleons that were due since
  many a day ;

And all Potosi's hoarded gold, and the wealth of half
    Peru,
Lay under the guns of Captain John, of Drake, and
    their English few.

So the governor manned his galley, and the Dons put
    out to greet
The long-expected vanguard as he deemed of the
    convoy fleet ;

But he found himself on an alien deck, and he stared
    at Captain John,
And he bowed a cold obeisance, and made haste to
    get him gone ;

While couriers sped fast inland to ride with the evil
    news,
There were heretics and pirate craft in the port of
    Vera Cruz.

Then stoutly smiled John Hawkins, and he said,
    "Sith need must be,
I will hold this port of the King of Spain till my
    ships can face the sea :

"By the chance of storm and our evil star we are
    here in the lion's jaw;
And here, my lads, we must hold our own by the need
    that knows no law!"

———

Now the haven pass is narrow, but it widens deep
    inland
From the isle which bars the entrance and the long
    low spit of sand;

So they warped their ships to the new sea-wall in the
    lee of the island south,
Where the lead gave seven fathoms, and they held
    San Juan's mouth.

And they landed guns on the island, they worked
    with might and main,
And they built the fort Defiance in the jaws of the
    King of Spain.

No moon betrayed their counsel as they laboured
    through the night,
And dawn broke over a freshening sea with the
    convoy fleet in sight.

There were six tall ships on the starboard line, and
 seven more on the port,
But the English flag was waving from a spar on the
 island fort.

So Don Alvarez de Bazan hove to outside the bar,—
It was he that took the London ships in the roads of
 Gibraltar ;

Who had ordered the flag of England to be trailed in
 his rudder's wake,
And the crews to the Holy Office for the galleys or
 the stake.

Then a boat shot out from the haven and drew to the
 flagship's lee,
John Hawkins sat in the stern-sheets, with his cutlass
 on his knee ;—

"To the Lord High Admiral greeting, for the peace
 that is between
King Philip's royal majesty and my own most gracious
 Queen ;

"We be English seamen weather-bound in a port of
    the King of Spain,
As we came in peace we would bide in peace, and in
    peace sail out again ;

"We met with a gale off Cuba, we are leaky and out
    of gear,—
But yet, my Lord, by your evil chance we are like to
    be masters here.

"There is one way into the haven, and that is a narrow
    way,
And not one ship can make it if I choose to say you
    nay ;

"If the breeze should freshen to half a gale, as it blew
    for a week and more,
You'll find no break five hundred miles in the surf on
    the long lee shore,—

"We hold the fort on the island bar, and I swear to
    you on my creed,
I will sink you all in the narrow pass if my warrant
    must be my need.

" But if you will pledge your honour in the name of
    the King of Spain
You will do my ships no violence so long as we shall
    remain,

" You will neither let nor hinder my men upon shore
    or sea,
And leave the ward of the island fort to my captains
    and to me ;

" If you sign these terms of treaty here under your
    hand and seal
Ye shall pass in peace to your moorings, and all shall
    be to your weal ;

" But if you will give me no such bond, in the name
    of England's Queen
I give you the bond of an Englishman that ye shall
    not enter in ! "

Then the face of Don Alvarez grew dark with an evil
    frown,
As his captains came about him and they paced it up
    and down ;

For he held the King's commission to chase and
    harry and take
The bodies of one John Hawkins and his kinsman
    Francis Drake.

The day wore by debating while the freshening north
    wind grew,
And the waves came crisply curling with a long white
    edge to the blue ;

The shrill breeze sang in the cordage, and panic grew
    with the wind,
He looked at the lee-shore breakers, he looked at the
    bond, and signed.

So the stately galleons entered between the isle and
    the crags,
While our men stood all to quarters and the Queen's
    ships dipped their flags.

The Spaniards moored in the inner port where the
    laden Plate Fleet lay,
The English bode by the new sea-wall, but the breeze
    died down with the day.

Then all went well for a little while, there was change
     of courtesies,
The men took heart of confidence and they landed
     on the quays ;

They marvelled much at the giant ships that were
     nigh two thousand tons,
With castles set on the poop and prow and tier over
     tier of guns :

Not all the fleet of England could have mustered
     such a line,
And they pledged the Dons in fellowship, and they
     tasted Spanish wine.

———

It was noon on the third day after, we had half of
     our crews away
When the sudden rattle of musket fire rang over the
     silent bay ;

The galleons slipped a cable's length and set nearer
     with the tide,
While a great black hulk towed seaward swang round
     to the *Minion's* side.

There was never a word of warning till the ships' sides
    clashed, and then
Their boarders sprang to the ratlins and the hulk
    grew quick with men;

But the war drums beat to quarters, and a cry went
    round our ships,
The crews sprang up the hatchways with "Treason!"
    on their lips;

And they snatched up pike and hatchet and capstan-
    bar and sword,
And they dashed out on the Spaniards, and they flung
    them overboard;

While stricken men with gaping wounds came swim-
    ming off from shore,
And boats put back in frantic haste to the ships they
    reached no more.

They hoisted sail in a hail of shot, and they cut the
    hawsers free,
So the *Minion* and the *Judith* won safe to the open
    sea.

But the *Jesus* lay dismantled where the galleons ringed
    her round,
And they opened fire at the stroke of noon in black
    San Juan's Sound.

The land troops crossed in barges by the shoals from
    the haven town,
They took the fort on the island, and they mowed the
    gunners down ;

They trained her guns on the *Jesus*, and she fought
    like a wolf at bay,
With the hound pack barking round her, cut off from
    the narrow way.

They will plead reserves of conscience, and the oath
    that is no oath,
But dearly Don Alvarez shall pay for his broken
    troth,—

For the gunners of the *Jesus* have laid their pieces
    true,
And they struck him hard on the water-line, and they
    lacked the flagship through ;

The wave rushed in by the breaches, and there rose a
    shuddering cry
From the soldiers penned in the fighting-decks to
    every saint in the sky,

The main-mast snapped and toppled with the banner
    of proud Castile,
The poop sank down in the churning sea, and the
    stem showed clean to the keel ;

While far away from the *Judith's* deck they answered
    a cheer that broke,
As the Admiral's great Armada went down in a cloud
    of smoke.

"So the devil comes to his own again !" laughed grim
    old Captain John,
And his blue eyes flashed through the powder smirch,
    as he roared from the poop, " Fight on !"

Then the galleys filled with boarders, and ever again
    they came,
With their muskets laid on the gunwale and their
    tow-pikes all aflame ;

D

But he dropped his main and fore yard, and he blocked
    his decks across,
And ever again the boarders went back to their shame
    and loss.

There were four great galleons silenced when the
    powder was spent at last,
When they loosed their fireships on him, and then the
    end came fast ;

So he manned his boats with the rest of his crew, and
    they cut their desperate way
To the harbour gate and the narrow strait and into
    the outer bay ;

And there as they won to the *Minion* and climbed to
    the *Judith's* decks,
They could see the *Jesus* burning in the midst of a
    ring of wrecks ;

And all the fruits of the voyage, the silver and gems
    and gold,
The charts they had made, and the traitor's bond, went
    down with the burning hold.

There was none that dared to follow of all they had
  fought so well,—
The kindlier sea received them and the shadow of
  evening fell.

———

Day broke on a dreary ocean, San Juan was far
  behind,—
And the God of the just and unjust tethered the wings
  of the wind.

So they hugged the reefs long days and nights, till
  they chanced on an inland reach,
Where the surf was still, and the lead sank deep, and
  the wave lay asleep on the beach;

Where the smooth transparent water was clear as a
  film of air,
Over fathom-deep weed gardens and sea things marvel-
  lous fair;

Where the forest pressed to the blue tide's marge, and
  never mayhap till then
Wide wandering ships had carried the venturous lives
  of men.

And a hundred souls of their own free will were left
  on the tropic shore,
Since they never might win to England with the
  burden that they bore.

Solemn was that leave-taking, where they knelt in the
  alien sand,
Commending these their comrades into their Maker's
  hand;

For a year and more in an alien world they had shared
  in weal and woe,
Had breasted storm and affronted toil, and had held
  their own with the foe;

And those rough old dogs of the ocean were tender of
  heart and true,
And comrade clung to his comrade staunch as captain
  clung to his crew;

There were salt wet tears on the furrowed cheeks that
  the tropic suns had tanned
As they bade farewell, and they left them there to their
  chance in an unknown land;

To an evil fate, and an unforeseen, as it proved in the
  years to be,
When the curse of the Holy Office fell over that island
  sea.

———

It was well-nigh three months later the watch on the
  Hoe descried
The wraith of a battered warship beat in on the flood-
  ing tide ;

Through the dismal wintry waters, through infinite
  trials past,
Hungry and lean and spent with storm, it was Drake
  come home at last.

And later yet in the new year's dawn came the little
  Minion too,
Smitten with plague in the ocean and manned with a
  stranger crew.

But the length and the breadth of England took fire
  at the news they brought,
The treason of Don Alvarez and the fight John
  Hawkins fought.

And Drake has got him another ship, and sworn to
    the Lord of Hosts
He will claim redress at the cannon's mouth round all
    their ports and coasts,

Till the treasure stores of the Indies have atoned to
    him fifty-fold
The loss of the good ship *Jesus* and her men and the
    Guinea gold ;

And so he has gathered a willing crew with the rest
    of his *Judith's* men,
And they're off once more on the same old trail, and
    it's Westward Ho again ;

And wherever the wide seas open he will brook no
    bar nor stay,
And there's never a wave but English sails shall claim
    for their free highway ;

Till the sceptre shall pass of ocean, and the whole of
    the world shall know
That an English life is a sacred thing wherever a
    keel can go !

And Captain John was on all men's lips, and his loss
    was England's gain,
For his single ship had shattered the myth of the
    might of Spain.

GREENAWAY

GREENAWAY

THE mother looked out from the window-bay, looked
    over the woods to the sea,
And, "Where are those three bonny boys of mine?"
    and "where are they gone?" said she.

The gardener's lad with the wave-tanned face looked
    up from the blush-rose bed,
"They have taken the boat and dropped on the ebb
    at dawn of the day," he said.

The mother turned from the window-bay, she was
    fair as three-months' bride,
" Ah well-a-day for my three wild boys and their lust
    of the sea," she sighed.

But deeper yet had the mother sighed, could she
　　know what the years would bring,
The gift of the sea, and the doom of the sea, and the
　　faith of a craven king.

A stone's throw under the windows by dale and
　　covert and down
The Dart winds home from its moorland source to
　　the roads and the haven town ;

And thither it was in an old sea-boat from their home
　　at Greenaway
The eager sons of the manor-house would fare for
　　their holiday ;

There were Humphry and Adrien Gilbert, with their
　　friend from over the moor,
The yeoman's son John Davies to tug at the heavy
　　oar,

And the lad that held the tiller, the fourth and
　　youngest one,
Was the heir of Walter Raleigh and the same fair
　　mother's son.

What deeds of wild adventure they have dared on
    that Devon stream
When the fabled West was an easy quest to a boy's
    light-hearted dream.

When the river-reach was their tropic sea, and the
    coast was the Spanish Main,
And the blistered wreck on the ebb-tide shoal was a
    great galleass of Spain.

And so they would come to the haven, where, moored
    to the laden quays,
Were the ships at rest with their canvas furled from
    a hundred marvellous seas;

The lofty poops and the painted hulls of the beauti-
    ful ships of old,
The carven prows and the open ports with their guns
    that shone like gold;

For the boys that were born and cradled where the
    breeze of the ocean blows,
They loved those ships with the passion that only the
    sea child knows.

And the Channel rovers knew them, the men of the
    western shire,
And told them tales of the ocean life and the world
    of a boy's desire ;

There was one that had sailed with Strangways,
    another with red Tremayne ;
They could tell of the Holy Office and the rule of
    the monk in Spain ;

Of the corsair folk in the eastern isles with the long
    brass guns on deck,
Of the north sea spray, of a gale in the bay, of a fight,
    of a run, of a wreck ;

Of the fur-clad folk and the frost-bound shores where
    the day and the night are one,
And the drifting ice-floes sparkle to the gleam of the
    midnight sun ;

But the tale that held them longest was the tale of
    the isles that lie
Far over the great Atlantic and the land of the sunset
    sky ;

Where veiled in rumour and fable, withdrawn as a
  virgin bride,
The world to be wooed and conquered was a quest
  that was still untried.

Then the lips would part and the eager eyes go westward over the sea,
"A little while, but a little while, and the time will
  come for me."

Now back—for the tide sets inland, and the mother
  frets in the hall,
"We have far to go ere the sun be low,—good hap to
  ye, masters all!"

"God speed to ye, gentle worships—good hap to ye,
  honest John,
Good luck to you, young Squire Raleigh, and keep
  your eye on the Don!"

The mother looked out as the westering sun went
  under the steep moor-side,
And "Where are those three bonny boys of mine?
  they are long from their home," she sighed.

But deeper yet had the mother sighed, could she
    know what the end would be,
For to all save one in the after years their doom came
    out of the sea.

THE REPRISAL

E

THE REPRISAL

Being the veracious narrative of John Killigrew, gentleman adventurer, who accompanied Captain Francis Drake on his second voyage to Darien ; done into the modern manner.

OH sweetly rang the Plymouth bells on the day we
    put to sea,
When May and June were nearly met and the new
    leaf on the tree ;

And sweetly over Edgcumbe's isle the setting sun
    declined,
It was Whitsun-Eve of May-time, and the May thrill
    in the wind.

There were hats that waved and kerchiefs, a cheer
    rang round the quays
As the fiddler played our anchors up and the new
    sails took the breeze.

The highlands drew their mantle round, and high up
    on the Hoe,
And nestling deep in shadowy hills red lights began
    to show ;

But the eager heart looked never back on a world so
    good to leave,
To the orchard lawns and the cowslip fields and the
    bells of Whitsun-Eve.

Our captain stood on the *Pasha's* poop as we won to
    the open sea ;
"Now lay her straight in the sunset track, for it's
    Westward Ho !" said he.

I sailed with Drake and with Oxenham, and the
    captain's brother John
With the rest of those who ventured were aboard of
    the little *Swan*.

We were three-and-seventy men and boys when the
    muster-log was told,
And only one of the seventy-three who was thirty
    summers old.

The crew were Dart and Plymouth men, with the four
    I brought from Looe,
Jack Basset and the Widdicombes, and my foster-
    brother Drew.

Two years were gone since the *Dragon* ship sailed
    out with the self-same men,
And Drake had won him his right of way to the Gulf
    of Darien ;

And the little *Swan* got an evil name last year on the
    Spanish Main,
For the long white wings of the tiny craft were a
    match for the best of Spain.

The breeze was fair, with the topsails square, and never
    a reef we flew,
And the heart of our little captain was a fire to the
    heart of his crew ;

It passed to a proverb in after-years with the men who
    had loved him well—
You were sure of heaven with Gilbert, but with Drake
    you had daunted Hell !

At last we had sight of the Windwards limned like a
  cloud in the sky,
It was five weeks out from the Lizard, and the second
  day of July;

And not in vain we had proved those seas and charted
  the reefs last year,
And laid the course by the star and sun that the
  venture had to steer,

For we saw strange sails to the eastward, and ran for
  a week of days
Past flowery cliffs where the blue wave winds through
  the calm of the island maze.

The men were mad to be landing, but he suffered it
  not to be
Till our track was lost in the wildering isles, and we
  struck on the Carib Sea.

We voided the path of traders, ran west yet awhile,
  and then
Bore down on the midmost channel of the Gulf of
  Darien;

And we came to the hidden haven he had found two
 years before,
We anchored under the high cliffs' lee, and at last we
 went ashore.

We felled the forest timbers and planted a high
 stockade,
Where they pieced the jointed pinnace under the
 ceiba's shade ;

While we shot the mark with the arquebus, we
 measured swords in play,
And Drake assigned the prizes that the Dons would
 have to pay ;

The chattering monkeys swarmed to watch and swung
 on the climbing vine,
The parrots screamed in the branches, but of man was
 never a sign.

A week from the day we landed they had launched
 three handy craft,
Twelve-oared and low in the water, and long with a
 shallow draft.

Their crews were picked and a course was buoyed as
　　the sun dropped low to the west,—
The Devon muscle was good to see on shoulder and
　　arm and chest,—

And the cliffs of the silent haven rang to the helms-
　　man's cries
As the *Minion* raced the *Jesus* and the *Judith* won the
　　prize,

When round the sheltering headland, traced black
　　on the even glow,
Came sailing in a barque of war with a caravel in
　　tow !

In a flash we were back to the *Pasha's* side, and
　　Oxenham, mighty of lung,
Hailed them over the waters, for he spoke with the
　　Spaniard's tongue ;

While the gunners stood to their pieces with linstocks
　　over the breech,
But the answer came in the *Devonshire* with a
　　" Plague on your foreign speech ! "

It was Rance the Channel rover in Sir Edmund
    Horsey's barque,
Grown tired of his privateering in the Downs with de
    la Mark;

And so he had sailed on fortune's wind right into the
    heart of the west;
And here was a man to our captain's hand, we were
    far too few at the best;

For the mettle of Drake had fired us, we were set on
    the wildest plan
That ever perchance had dazzled the desperate dreams
    of man;—

On the coast due east from Nombre lay a cluster of
    isles he knew
Girded in reefs and white with shoals that had
    daunted an older crew;

He would hide his ships in the wooded isles, and
    thence with a chosen band
Creep on by night in the launches under the lee of
    land;

He would enter the port of Nombre, the great treasure-
    house of Spain,
And carry a year's gold harvest back to his ships
    again.

So a bond was made and a treaty signed, and the forty
    with Rance were sworn
To stand by Drake in the venture, and we sailed with
    the break of morn.

We came to the fir-grown islands—we sounded wary
    and slow
Till we found a way through the sunken rocks where
    the ships might pass in tow,

And we laid them up in a shore-locked bay that ran
    like a lake inland,
With the world-old forest ringing the rim of its silver
    sand ;

We drew the lot and we started, night through we
    tugged at the oar,
Seventy men in the launches, and with day drew in to
    the shore ;

We fought with the surf and conquered, we slept
    through the sultry noons,
We woke with the shadow of evening and toiled by
    the waning moons ;

Till the fifth sun sank in a stormy sky, and at last the
    launches lay
Adrift on a murky midnight off the point of Nombre
    bay.

We knew that beyond that headland a world-famed
    city slept,
And closer yet with a muffled stroke the four swift
    launches crept.

Great clouds shut out the starlight, the moon would
    be late to rise,
There was one black void of water under one black
    void of skies ;

Far off the long surf thundered on an unseen shingle
    shore,
And between its measured pulse-beats you felt the
    silence more ;

And the awe of the shifting darkness wrought into
    each straining sense
Till you heard your own heart beating in the stillness
    of suspense.

Then eastward rose a glimmer as it might be, faint
    and dim,
The first white touch of dawning over the ocean rim.

It was only the moon belated, but " Yonder," he said,
    " comes day,
One last pull round the headland and Drake will
    show the way ! "

There was hardly a light in Nombre but the lamp at
    the haven head,
And away beyond at the landing-place where the
    cresset fires shone red ;

So we stole in under the shadow at the edge of the
    new sea-wall,
While the moon sailed up through a cloudy bank and
    we heard the sentry call ;

There were ten men left in the launches, there were
    threescore sprang to the land,
And we rushed to the fort at the haven mouth and
    tumbled the guns in the sand;

But the gunners dropped in the fosses and fled
    through the night unhurt,
And they roused the sleepy watchmen, and the dark-
    ness grew alert:

The great bell tolled from the belfry, it clanged with
    an eerie stroke,
And rumour swelled to a stormy cry as the shuddering
    city woke;

For Drake had carried the market-place, and the
    guards were full in flight
As I fell on their flank with Oxenham, and panic
    screamed in the night,—

We charged with a babel of horn and drum, we yelled
    our rallying cry,
And the torches fixed on our ten-foot pikes blazed
    into the murky sky.

So we fought our way to the treasure-house, and the
    guards fell back once more,
The bowmen kept them at bow-shot length while we
    rammed through the iron door,

And we stared on an Empire's ransom in the torch-
    light's glare, untold
Wedges of silver shoulder high and the Inca's virgin
    gold.

There were gems imbedded in rough-hewn quartz
    that caught the flickering gleam,
There were pearls to be had for the snatching, wealth
    over our wildest dream !

But the great Church bell of Nombre boomed on
    with its call to arms,
And we heard their war-drums beating and the bugles'
    shrill alarms,

We heard the rattle of musket fire where our boats
    were left behind,
While clouds rolled over the moon again and a chill
    struck into the wind ;

"They never must form to rally, back, lads, to the
market-place!"
And lo! as he sprang to lead us our captain fell on
his face:

Long since he had gotten a grisly wound, and his
strength had ebbed as it bled,
But our hearts stood still for a moment's space at the
thought he had fallen dead;

For a sudden volley had struck the ground, and the
sand splashed into our eyes
As we staggered blind from the lightning-flash shot
over the purple skies:

Then the tropic rain burst o'er us, and our matchlock
fires were drenched,
Our bow-strings would not serve us, and the blazing
tow was quenched;

We raised our wounded captain, and we bore him
back to the quay,
While he cursed us all for cravens—"Will you lose
this chance?" said he.

But his men with a gentle violence had forced him
    out of the strife,
For all the gold in the west, they said, was as naught
    to their captain's life.

So the Spanish footmen rallied, and the streets grew
    live with men,
And we fought with the pike and the musket-butt,
    and we charged them one to ten.

We laid our wounded under the thwarts with the
    spoil we had brought away,
And never a man was missing as we pushed out into
    the bay.

We climbed on board of a seventy-ton, and we cut
    the hawsers free,
We towed her out, and we hoisted sail, and made for
    the open sea.

While day-dawn scowled through a sullen sky, and
    ever our captain railed,
"Had I been quit of my wound," he said, "the
    venture had not failed."

But we found good store on the captured ship of red
    and of amber wines,
And our wounds were nigh forgotten when we came
    to the isle of pines.

So Rance took his share of the Nombre gold, and the
    barque sailed home again,
And that was the first reprisal that we made in the
    Spanish Main.

———

Then we sailed to Cartagena, and we ran right up the
    port,
'Mid clanging of bells from the churches, and
    thunder of guns from the fort ;

And the launches dashed through the musket fire,
    and under the Governor's eyes
Laid hands on a Cadiz transport, and carried her out
    a prize.

He sent the prisoners back to shore in their boats for
    his good name's sake,
For there never was gentler pirate or kindlier foe than
    Drake ;

F

But he freed the slaves we had found on board at
    work in collar and chain,

And thus we won to our service these the deadliest
    foes of Spain.

It was first at Cartagena we were 'ware of the evil
    news

That the men of the Holy Office had landed in Vera
    Cruz.

They told us of our good comrades in the hands of a
    ruthless foe,

The *Judith's* men and the *Minion's* that were left
    three years ago ;

And they told us four great galleons had sailed in the
    Pasha's track

Because of the raid on Nombre, with an oath to bring
    us back.

So we made as though we were eastward bound, and
    scuttled the little *Swan*

On the rocks near Cartagena, and with nightfall we
    were gone.

We were sore at heart for the brave little craft, but
    our hands were all too few
To work one ship with the prizes and to man the
    launches too.

So we turned and steered for a lonely bay, far out of
    their mariners' ken,
He had found in a deep reef-sheltered blue elbow of
    Darien :

Long creeks run up from its shelving shore to the
    foot of the hills inland,
Where the rain-born torrents cleave a way through
    the mud swamps and the sand ;

Where over the banks untrodden, in mist and in
    fever-breath,
The silent mangrove forest broods on a world of
    death ;

Their black stems rise from the waters, their thin bent
    roots divide,
And clutch with uncanny fingers the drift of the
    shifting tide ;—

We hid our ships in the gloomy creeks, with their
  topmasts stowed away,
And we built us huts on the upland, with an outlook
  over the bay.

It were long to tell of the raids we made from our
  lair in Plenty Cove,
How we built a fort at the forest edge, and our every
  venture throve ;

For thence the swift black launches would creep
  through the island maze,
By the channels still uncharted to the edge of the
  great highways,

They would board the coastwise traders becalmed
  on the tropic nights,
They claimed sea-toll from the victualling ships and
  fought in a hundred fights ;

But we paid the price of rashness, when at last on an
  evil day
With a weary stroke and a bleeding crew the boats
  crawled back to the bay

With the tale of a raid too well repelled, of the few
    that were far too few,
With the mangled bodies of Captain John and my
    foster-brother Drew.

We dug their graves in the alien world, as a sailor's
    grave should be,
On a spur of the hill at the forest edge where it looks
    to the open sea;

And we mourned as you mourn for the first to fall,
    and there stole on the brooding mind
A thought of the lights last Whitsun-Eve and of all
    we had left behind.

———

Now the slaves we had freed and friended were gone
    forth to the jungle folk,
The fierce black tribes of the Cimaroons with the
    links of the chain we broke,

A symbol of peace and friendship, that their great
    cacique might know
The men of the woods and the men of the sea were
    at war with a common foe;

They were sprung, they claimed, from the mutineers
  that had once been a galley's crew,
And a deadly hate of their lords of old was the only
  law they knew ;

They had got them wives of the Indian folk, and
  here on the free hillside,
In the tracking of game and the plunder of man, they
  had thriven and multiplied.

So the chiefs came down to our camping ground, and
  the tribe abode with us there,
And we learned the lore of their forest craft, and the
  trick of the woodman's snare.

They told us priceless tidings, how the rains were
  near at hand,
When the hill streams grew in the torrent beds and
  travel is barred by land,

But so we would wait in our hiding-place till the dry
  months came again,
When the plate stores cross from the southern sea to
  the ports on the Spanish Main ;

They would guide us over the jungle waste through
    the crags by an unknown way
To the path of the laden mule-trains, and the road to
    Nombre Bay.

So the rains came on in their season, and the hills
    raced down to the seas,
And ever it poured on our cranky thatch, and it
    dripped in the night of the trees;

The weeks went by in a shadow of gloom till the
    camp was a dismal fen,
Till the chill of the rain wrought into our souls, and
    the heart died out of our men.

Then the gray skies broke and the sun pierced through,
    but the white mist rose like a shroud
From the ooze and slime of the mangrove creek, and
    death was abroad in the cloud.

And one by one in the fever camp our men dropped
    down and died;
There were twenty-and-nine of the seventy-three that
    are laid there side by side;

Till we cursed the sea and the hoarded gold, and the
toil we had spent for its sake ;
But stronger than death, and the fear of death, was
the quenchless heart of Drake.

Though his youngest brother, the lad we loved,
dropped down in his strength and prime,
And I saw great tears in the stern blue eyes for the
first and only time,—

Yet he came and went with a cheery smile, he sat by
each sick man's bed,
He nerved the doubting surgeons, and at night bore
out his dead.

We dug him a grave by Captain John at the head of
that line of mounds,—
They will rise up first on the judgment dawn when
the last great muster sounds ;

They will call their lads to quarters, and my foster-
brother Drew
Will pipe on his boatswain's whistle that the men of
the *Pasha* knew,

And I pray the Lord have mercy, when the angel
  reads the scrolls,
For the bitter death that they died out there, on those
  poor seamen's souls.

For look you it is sweet and well in the day we come
  to die,
To know familiar presences and kindred faces by;

To watch from sheltering windows wide the happy
  light that plays
On pleasant scenes that seem to soothe the ebbing of
  our days;

To see the shadows lengthening down the quiet fields
  we knew,
And the farewell sunset purpling the distant hills of
  blue;

While tender voices whisper near with gently bated
  breath,
So softly in its season falls the kindly kiss of death.

But it's ill to pass in the wilderness on the bed of
wattled reeds,

With only the swamp to cool the fire of the fever that
it breeds.

Yet they that march in England's van have such grim
death to face,

And alien suns shall bleach the skulls of our unquiet
race.

The desert wastes shall gather them, the red sand
choke their groans,

And every tide of all the seas roll up their restless
bones.

———————

So there we endured and conquered, the evil drew
to an end,

The murmur hushed in his greater loss, and the sick
began to mend.

And yet we were hardly a score in all that were strong
to march and fight,

When the scouts brought news from Nombre of the
Plate fleet hove in sight;

But thirty men of the Cimaroons marched out with
    their great cacique,
And they suffered us bear no burdens from the day
    we left the creek.

We struck through the gloom of the forest, where the
    dark arms tangle and cross,
And the weird dead trunks rot slowly under their pall
    of moss,

Where there dwells eternal silence and never the sun-
    light breaks
The roof that tents the twilight of a sleep where no
    life wakes.

They found us a track where no track was, and we
    crept on their noiseless trail
Through the steamy shade and the fungus slime to
    the world of a fairy tale;

We climbed the Cordilleras, up steps of the mountain
    rills
That yet ran full with the overflow from the springs
    in the heart of the hills;

We passed through untrodden valleys where the
  shrubs had an odour of balm,
And the wild wood creatures dwelt unscared in the
  old primeval calm ;

The sap of those trees ran white like milk, the wounds
  in the bark ran blood,
The fruit hung luscious on every bough, and the ripe
  fruit grew by the bud ;

The cotton blanched in a silky tuft, the bamboos
  waved their flags,
The acacia pods were a sabre's length, and the wild
  gourd clung to the crags.

We came to a break in the mountain chain at end
  of a weary day,
A pass hewn deep in the great rock wall, and the late
  moon rose that way ;

The upland hollow was dense with bush, and the
  grass rose shoulder high,
There was nought to see for its forest ring but the
  stars far up in the sky ;

And lone in the jungle clearing one monster ceiba
    stood,
The last of a race of giants of the patriarchal wood;

Its wide arms stretched to the rock's high crest, and
    its branches bar on bar
Were the rungs of a mighty ladder that reached right
    up to the star;

The great lianes wound through them and drooped
    to the earth again,
And myriad blooms of orchids had life from the
    living chain;

They pitched our camp in the mighty roots, and they
    waved their hands on high,
And they said, "Climb up, Señores, for this is the
    Mountain's Eye!"

So Drake swung up through the creepers, and he
    scaled the ancient tree,
And first of all living Englishmen had a sight of the
    Golden Sea.

Beneath him forests lay in gloom, dim gorges wound
   between
White crags like billows cresting in the moonlight's
   marble sheen.

Behind the vast Atlantic rolled, and widening glimmering west
The sister ocean rose and took the moon-kiss on her
   breast.

He clambered down with a bursting heart, and fell on
   his bended knee,
And awe came over us all who watched, and he said,
   "Go up and see!"

And I went aloft through the twisted coils, and
   Oxenham climbed, and then
The mariners each went up in turn to the last of the
   Pasha's men:

And the mystic secret was no more hid, and the
   jealous lords of Spain
Had veiled the face of the virgin sea, and had barred
   her gates in vain!

We stood ringed round together, bared heads by the
    flickering fire,
We sang the "Nunc Dimittis," and Jack Basset led
    the choir;

And we swore the oath of a fellowship in the shade
    of the ceiba tree,
We would never rest till an English keel had sailed
    on the Golden Sea.

Then we dropped down the gorges, and we came on
    the second day
To the meeting of roads in a mountain pass, and they
    said, "There winds the way!"

And we looked once more on the western sea, and
    saw from the ridge afar
The fleets of the sister ocean in the roads of Panama.

The black folk sent their scouts to spy while the noon
    was sultry yet,
And they saw the mule-trains gathered to march when
    the sun should set.

So we chose a place in the level way and the narrow
    strait of the pass,
Between the gates of the east and west, and hid in
    the jungle grass;

And there we had ease of our weariness as we lay by
    twos and threes
Through the trance of the burning noontide in shadow
    of rocks and trees.

They rolled us leaves of a priceless herb that grew in
    their hill domain,
Whose fumes are better than meat and drink, a drug
    to the heart and brain;

And our limbs worn out with the mountain march
    were soothed with a sweet relief
As our lips inhaled its fragrance, and our souls forgot
    their grief.

Then the sun went down on the western sea, the stars
    in the east grew bright,
And the fireflies lit their lanterns in the sudden tropic
    night;

And since the moon would be late to rise each man
    drew on his shirt
Outside of his seaman's jersey, and we lay by our
    arms alert.

There were twenty men in the ambush with the breast-
    high grass for screen,
On either side of the mountain track, and a bow-shot's
    length between.

The drowsy night air hummed with life, the forest
    things gave tongue,
While measured on the throbbing pulse the minutes
    dragged along.

Then far and faint on rustling breaths that seemed to
    move in sleep,
We could hear the mule bells tinkle far down the
    misty deep ;

And ever they mounted nearer, till we heard the hide-
    whips crack,
Till the echoes rang with the jangling chime, and the
    hoofs that slipped on the track.

G

They hummed an air as they rode along, the guards
    at the head of the line,
They rode right into the ambush, and then Drake
    gave the sign ;

And the night was rent with a wild war-cry, the bolt
    rang keen from the bow,
The black men sprang to the pack-mules' heads,
    and we all dashed out on the foe.

The escort stood for one moment's space in the jungle
    path at bay,
And then fled clattering madly back, or on to Nombre
    Bay.

And we loosed the packs, and we lashed the mules
    behind them left and right,
And headlong down the desperate paths they galloped
    through the night.

But all the cost of our voyage was paid us a thousand-
    fold
In the gems we took from the rifled packs and the
    red Potosi gold ;

And as for the silver ingots that we had no hands
to bear,
We stuffed them into the crannied rocks and under
the tree-roots near.

Then we clambered up by the hill-stream's course,
though the way was dark to find,
Where our feet on the dripping boulders would leave
no trail behind.

We were far away on the mountain's crest before the
alarm had spread,
When dawn broke rosy wakening out of her ocean
bed ;

For panic grew with the morning light, gave wings
to the evil news,
And they landed guns from the ships of war, and
they armed at Venta Cruz.

And still folks say that in Panama you may hear the
settlers tell
How the Dragon came in his devil-ship, and he made
a league with hell ;

For their own guards saw the black fiends swarm
    and gather at his call,
And they cross themselves as they tell the tale :
    " From such God save us all ! "

But we went down by the pathless crags through the
    thorn-brakes' tangled coil,
Where the face of the cliff was sheerest, bent under
    the weight of spoil ;

And we came to the edge of the ocean at eve on the
    second day,—
Our hearts were glad for the salt waves' smell and
    beat of the tossing spray,—

We came to the gorge with its winding stream where
    our trysting-place should be,
And there were our launches hidden in a sheltered
    arm from the sea;

And there were our comrades waiting, grown hearty
    and hale once more,
And wild at the sight of the treasure loads that our
    black companions bore.

We gave the chiefs to their hearts' desire of our arms
    and stores and loot,
And we left them all the launches and a Spanish
    prize to boot ;

And we got on board of our own good ship, made
    trial of spar and mast,
Streamed all the silken pennants and shook sail out
    at last.

We skirted Cartagena with the red cross at our main,
To fire one last defiance to King Philip and to Spain;

And gaily through the tropic sea we ran before the
    wind,
And left the name of Francis Drake and the fear of
    God behind.

Oh sweetly rang the Sabbath bells across from shore
    to shore
The merry August morning when we sighted home
    once more ;

We heard them ring to matins from Cawsand and the
    Rame,
And sweetly up the off-shore wind the homely voices
    came.

We thundered out our last salute to the Admiral of
    the Port,
And old John Hawkins answered with the guns in
    Plymouth fort.

And how the folks streamed out of church, and hurried
    down the Hoe,
And left the parson preaching, all lads in Plymouth
    know.

So there, my sons, the tale must end of what we did
    afloat,
You must ask good Master Walsingham what Philip's
    envoy wrote.

They say Mendoza still protests—and long he may
    in vain,—
But Spain will pause before she breaks her solemn
    bond again.

THE WORLD ENCOMPASSED

THE WORLD ENCOMPASSED

1

IT was summer now in the world they knew, mid June
    and the month of mirth,
But Drake was stayed in the winter's grip on the
    dreariest coast of earth.

They had sailed in a bleak November and assembled
    in Mogador,
He had taken a prize of the Portingals and had set
    her crew on shore :

He had made the Brazils in April and watered in
    River Plate,
And now two months he had sought in vain for the
    pass to Magellan's Strait.

In fog and in heavy weather, through wildering sleet
    and snow,
They had fought with the leaden waters in a track
    where no ships go,

Where the storm wind howls with a human voice,
    where the long swell flings its spray
Up cliffs where never a green leaf breaks the gloom
    of the wintry gray;

And still it blew from the frozen pole, and they beat
    in the icy breath,
The *Pelican* and the *Marygold* and the barque *Elizabeth.*

The heart of his men was broken, and ever the discord
    grew,
And a haunting dread of that unknown world crept
    over his simple crew;

Till they wrought with a grudging labour, till they
    answered with sullen lips,
And the breath of a mutinous murmur went up from
    the weary ships.

But the general watched and waited till the time
    should be ripe for speech ;
Till the hidden evil had come to light, and the
    sickness craved the leech.

They had won to an inlet isle-enclosed, by the reckon-
    ing fifty south,
And the battered fleet put in at last through the reefs
    that barred its mouth.

There were spars to be refitted, and the standing
    gear was worn,
The hulls were foul from the long sea-way, and the
    sails were frayed and torn.

There was never a ship sailed here but once, and now
    it was fifty years
Since the great Magellan anchored and dealt with his
    mutineers ;

There was never a trace of living thing in that arm
    of the lonely sea,
But high on the cliff in the silent world stood the
    frame of his gallows tree ;

And there, clean picked of the vultures, and washed
    by the driving rain,
The bones of a man swung to and fro held up in a
    rusty chain.

They stared at the silent witness of the great sea-
    captain's hand,
And the sense of an ill-foreboding came up from that
    dismal strand.

Now once more here at this world's far end among the
    boulders gray
Shall a court be called for judgment in bleak St.
    Julian's Bay.

For at last the leech has probed the wound and the
    bitter charge is framed,
Long-hidden things shall come to light and the
    traitor's name be named.

So Drake has called his captains and the mates and
    the volunteers,
And Master Thomas Doughty shall be tried before
    his peers ;

As ran the law in England, so ran their law at sea,
Who stood within its danger might claim his due
degree.

The chaplain brought the book to kiss, and swore
them man by man,
And grimly that mid-winter morn the ocean court
began.

Then witness after witness rose, and they told the
sordid tale
Of all the arts the man had used to make the venture
fail ;

Till the damning charge of his mutiny was established
to the hilt,
And that reluctant jury gave their verdict of his guilt.

But he, since Drake so humbled him, replied with
taunt and jest,
And by his own lips' railing stood a traitor self-
confessed ;

There were those at home in England of the counter-
plot, said he,
Who knew the end of this fool's design long ere they
had put to sea :

King Philip had ambassadors to guard the rights of
Spain,
And when the watchman waketh the wolf will prowl
in vain.

Then the eyes of Drake grew cold and hard with the
glance it was ill to meet,
And he called the crews together to the least man in
the fleet ;

From first to last he had said no word till then for
good or ill—
As he faced his wavering captains while his trumpet
blew the 'still.'

He stood erect in the midst of all with his drawn
sword in his hand
At the foot of Magellan's gallows by the edge of the
dreary land,

While the chill wind moaned in the gully and the
waves boomed far away
On the sunken reefs and the broken crags at the gate
of the wintry bay.

And he said : "My masters, hearken, friends old and
comrades new,
While I tell you all that my purpose holds and the
thing we have sailed to do.

"There was no man questioned whither on the day
we set to sea,
I am used to be trusted all in all by the men that sail
with me ;

"But your discords, aye and your mutinies, have left
me nigh distraught,
I must have this left, my masters, though the price be
dearly bought ;

"I would have you know that the gentlemen shall
take their place with the crew,
Shall haul and draw with the seamen when their
captain bids them to ;

" I will brook no more division—I would know who
    dares refuse.
God's life ! am I not your master ?—I will break you
    all if I choose !

" Let the *Pasha's* men stand forward, yon five that
    were with me then,
When we looked across to the unknown side from
    the tree in Darien.

" Do you mind my oath in the camp-fire light, how I
    swore, God helping me,
I would sail a ship with an English flag through the
    heart of the Golden Sea !

" Since then five years have come and gone, and now,
    so He hath willed,
The oath that I swore in Darien shall surely be ful-
    filled.

" For it fell in the time appointed that the Queen,
    whom God defend,
Had heard her subjects' bitter cry from Berwick to
    Land's End :

"And since the Spanish King protests his arm may
not control

The Holy Office in his realm, which lie be on his
soul,

"Since in the councils of her peers she had found
small help or stay,

And still unchallenged at her feet the King's defiance
lay ;

"So in her bitter need she turned from the grave and
proved, and wise,

And she called a poor sea-captain who had found
grace in her eyes.

"And thus it chanced upon a day, a year gone by and
more,

There came a summons to the court from the great
who guard her door.

"A hand put back the arras and beckoned round the
screen,

And I was kneeling at the feet of England's injured
Queen.

H

"She stood against the oriel frame and looked me up
　　and down,

Who wondered how so frail a brow could bear so
　　great a crown :

"'And this is Captain Francis Drake, and that the
　　guilty head

My kinsman Philip long hath craved, and craveth
　　still,' she said.

"She won my heart with mild reproof—with frowns
　　that died in smiles,

She learned the tale of all we did beyond the western
　　isles ;

"She hearkened and she never tired as I told it all
　　again,

How we stripped the mules at Nombre and scared
　　the Spanish Main :

"And then herself, with broken voice, she spake of
　　all her woes,

The peace proclaimed where no peace is, the bitter
　　cry that rose

" From cities where her merchant fleets lie idle by the
    quays
With rotting sail and fouling keel debarred from half
    the seas,

" From little havens in the cliffs, where their mothers
    watch in vain
For the lads that the fever dungeons will never yield
    again,

" From wretches maimed in torture cells, whose bodies
    show the scar
Where peace has struck the craven stroke they had
    never brooked in war,

" From those an alien judge hath doomed, and who
    for conscience' sake
Were greater than their fear of death and English at
    the stake,—

" And womanlike she sighed and said, ' And is there
    none to aid ? '
And queenly with a burst of scorn, ' Are all but I
    afraid ? '

"So there and then with halting breath, but all the
brain on fire,
I told our glorious Lady Liege of all my heart's desire.

"I told her of the great South Sea, the secret of our
foe,
Where unperceived of prying eyes his Plate-fleets
come and go,

"How there the sword he wields so well, the serried
pikes of Spain,
The guns that menace every sea are wrought for
England's bane,

"Where drowsy waves and laggard winds waft up to
Panama
The spoils of all the mines that sleep beneath the
summer star :

"And so the glorious scheme was planned to raid
the Golden Sea,—
Now let me know who turns his back on England
and on me !

"Still southlier yet through seas unsailed Magellan
found the gate
Where the sister oceans meet and mix at war in the
stormy strait :

"And though it shall blow ten times as wild, though
the pass be blind with snow,
Though its whirlpools spin with the drifted ice,—
where he went I will go ;

"Though the foul fiend have dominion there as the
seamen's fables say,
Though the devil in hell would hold me back,—I
have sworn to find the way ;

"But when we have won to the farther side, to the
breeding seas of the seal,
We shall sail on the gentlest ocean that ever has rocked
a keel :

"For these crags that freeze on the eastward face
slope green to the western blue
And a land breeze gently northing bears up for rich
Peru.

"There, where the treasure galleons ply secure from
  all attack,
Drop down to Valparaiso and bring the bullion back,

"I look to find the ransom that will more than buy
  again
The lives of all the English lads that rot to death in
  Spain.

"Then when the lockers burst with gems, and when
  the ballast hold
Of every ship in this my fleet is packed with bars of
  gold,

"We'll trust the luck of the sun's wake still, and it's
  Westward Ho once more,
And home, my lads, by an ocean-track ship never
  has tried before !

"Now if I have told you only here what but I and
  my captains knew,
It was that I learned in Venta Cruz of the harm loose
  tongues may do ;

"Therefore whoso hath no stomach to bear hand in
    this emprise,
Hath welcome and leave to take his choice as it
    seemeth best in his eyes;

"Let him go aboard of the *Marygold*—let him steer
    for home this day,—
But look to it whoso chooseth that he steer no other
    way;

"For I swear to you as God liveth, wherever my bark
    be blown,
I will sink his ship if I meet him, though he be of
    my blood and bone."

It was Captain Philip Wynter first of the barque
    Elizabeth
Stept forth and clasped the general's hand, and he
    said, "For life and death!"

And Thomas Moon the carpenter, the oldest hand at
    sea,
Spake up and swore a grisly oath, "Lord do so unto
    me,

" If ever a skulk shall turn his back while I have a
　　　head to break
On the spoiling of the Philistine and my Captain
　　　Francis Drake ! "

And there rose from twice a hundred throats a mighty
　　　English cheer,
That voice of hearts in unison the sea-queen loves to
　　　hear.

And Doughty heard it far away where he paced the
　　　lonely shore,
He heard and knew his doom was sealed—but the
　　　general spake once more ;

He said they were timid surgeons who were loth to
　　　use the knife,—
He spoke of their state endangered by their jealousies
　　　and strife,

Of the rule of ocean broken with brawls and mean
　　　affrays,
Of the slights put on the seamen, contentions, doubt,
　　　dispraise ;

And all that smouldering discontent had rallied round
    one name,
And the very hand he had trusted most was the hand
    that fanned the flame ;

Gentle and brave he had deemed him of old, of pur-
    pose steady and pure,
Master of manifold learning, venturous, strong to
    endure ;

But for all the love he had borne him once, yet he
    dared not be untrue
To the Queen's high expectation and the safety of his
    crew,

And so since warnings naught availed, and the evil
    might not mend,
He had called a court in judgment on his own
    familiar friend :

And there they had heard from his lips confessed the
    bond he had pledged to the foe,
The trust betrayed and the plot to bring this scheme
    to its overthrow.

"Henceforth," he said, "the watchman wakes, the foe
    has a thousand eyes,
And wealth and fame, or the gallows-tree, are the end
    of this emprise :

"Let no man look for quarter, henceforth who sails
    with Drake,
I warn him, if the voyage fail, his life will pay the
    stake ;

"Henceforth we are bound on a venture that is well-
    nigh past my wit,
We have set three kings by the ears, my lads, and we
    needs must through with it ;

"Howbeit I trust that the galleons will cruise on our
    trail in vain,
For we shall fare by the southern pass while they
    watch by the western main :

"But there waits one doom for treason at sea as it is
    on land,—
Who deems his crime has been worthy death let him
    hold forth his hand !"

Then a murmur rose from the listening ranks, an
    oath, and an angry cry,
And twice a hundred clenching fists condemned the
    wretch to die.

The crowd fell back, the general passed to where
    Doughty strode aloof—
Henceforth in all his words and deeds might no man
    find reproof;

He had played the stake for life or death as a gambler
    throws the cast,
And so, like a gallant gentleman, he would bear him
    to the last:

He heard his doom with fearless eyes, he doffed his
    hat to say,
"My cause be with the Judge of hearts until that
    latter day!"

He craved no grace save such an end as his gentle
    blood might bear,
To have his dues as a Christian man, and to shrive
    his soul in prayer.

So it came to pass on the second day that the crews
    were called ashore,
And they spread a banquet near the strand of the best
    they had in store ;

And there, unseen in the chill gray dawn, high up on
    a crest of rock,
In the face of Magellan's gallows-tree, Tom Moon set
    up the block :

They dressed an altar near at hand with the red cross
    banner spread,
Where the chaplain, stoled and surpliced, set on the
    wine and bread :

And Drake and Thomas Doughty knelt down there
    side by side,
In Nature's vast and awful shrine above the yellow
    tide,

While Master Fletcher ministered and blessed the
    bread and brake,
And gave the cup in brotherhood to Doughty and to
    Drake.

And those rough souls were awed and cowed, while
moaned the rainy wind,

And the deep voice of ocean boomed its measured
chant behind.

Then the long quarrel reconciled each kissed the
other's cheek,

And held his hand for a little space, but no man
heard them speak.

So they passed to where the feast was spread in a
sheltered spot to lee,

They made good cheer together there, each after his
degree.

But Doughty filled a cup and cried a pledge in
Spanish wine,

"Here's luck in all your ventures, lads, and a better
end than mine!"

And in a little while he rose, and with a courtier's
bow,

"With your good leave, my captain," he said, "I am
ready now."

They climbed the crest of broken hill to where the
    block was set,
As men unmoved by craven fear, by passion or regret.

And Doughty passed along the ranks with a word to
    each and all,
And as he knelt to try the block the rain began to
    fall.

But Drake unclasped his seaman's cloak and spread it
    on the ground,
And bared the sword his arm alone might wield in
    honour bound ;

The shivering blade whirled round and fell cold,
    cruel, swift and keen.
"So perish all her enemies!" said Drake; "God save
    the Queen !"

He spread his cloak about the corse, and raised the
    severed head,
The shuddering crews drew slowly back and left him
    with the dead :

And long he gazed in that pale face he shielded from
    the rain,
Thereafter, saith the chronicle, Drake seldom smiled
    again.

The grave is on that bleak foreshore, and the crime is
    purged away,
But steadfast stands while England stands her ocean
    law, "obey!"

II

Yet many a week they lingered there till their craft
    were fit for sea,
From stem to stern-post caulked and payed, for the
    fierce fight yet to be:

And they double-braced the standing-gear, reshipped
    their spars and stores,
And late in the wintry August took leave of those
    barren shores.

It was noon on the third day after, they had sight of
    the ocean gate
Where the long black wall of mountain is cleft by the
    fabled strait,

They saw the headlands break the swell, the great
    walls yawning wide,
And up the foam of shoaling reefs a path of steely
    tide ;

Thereat he streamed his banners out, and as he passed
    between
Drake struck his topsails on the bunt in homage to
    the Queen ;

And since his bird of wilderness had met with fortune's
    wind,
New named henceforth the *Pelican* shall sail the
    Golden Hind.

Their track wound in through narrowing gulfs with
    bastioned walls o'erbowed,
'Neath drifted snows on the dripping shelves and a tent
    of inky cloud :

Fierce wind-flaws drave with an angry blast at the turns
    of the winding way,
Bleak breaths that swept from the misted crags and
    lashed the freezing spray ;

Wild currents raced through the twisting tides that
    washed round wilderness isles,
And the shadow of night hung all day long in the deep
    scarred rock defiles ;

And ever at even wandering fires showed glimmering
    through the gloom,
While prisoned deep in the tunnelled caves they heard
    the pent seas boom ;

There many a stout heart shook for dread that had
    feared no earthly foe,
For the weird of night is an awesome thing in the
    paths where seamen go.

There was never a creek they moored in but the
    penguins ran in flocks
To stare at the strange intruders that climbed on their
    nesting rocks ;

And at times the strait way broadened out till the
    white mists hid the shore,
And they drifted on in a veil of fog till they heard the
    breakers roar,

Then the lead would fly from the sounding-chains, and
    the starboard line raced free,
While the larboard caught on a sunken edge of the
    shoal they might not see :

They were fifteen days and fifteen nights in the throat
    of the dismal strait,
And the shadow of death was near alway, but as yet
    they could smile at fate,

For ever the eye of the master watched, and a master-
    hand was laid
To sail and tiller and sounding gear, and a master-
    voice obeyed ;

Till the dreary battle was all behind, and at last the
    deed was done,
And the keel of an English ship ran out on the sea of
    the setting sun.

They watched him drop to the ocean rim, and they
    felt the old sea-spell
As with joy they beat to the open wave, and the long
    south twilight fell.

But lo, when the dawn came gray with cloud there
  was no more land on the lee,
And they met the tail of the western gale that is lord
  in the southern sea ;

And a tempest rose such as never yet they had hoped
  for heart to brave,
These men who had spent their whole hard lives at
  the chance of the evil wave.

It flung them south and it drave them east, while the
  mountain tides ran past
With death in the hiss of the breaking swell and death
  in the boom of the blast ;

The sky pressed down on their bare mast poles as they
  scudded before the wind,
As they climbed the seas and shuddered at the sheer
  green gulfs behind ;

And swiftlier raced the following tide with the white
  comb reared to whelm,
And they knew how nigh was the dread lee-shore, but
  they dared not change the helm.

The nights grew brief in that wintry world, but there
  broke no friendly sun
Through the cumbered cloud and the drifting scud,
  and the night and the day seemed one.

So ever they toiled at the creaking pumps and the
  breach that the green seas made,
And ever they cried on the Lord of Storms, and their
  hearts were unafraid.

Week after week at the tempest's will the *Golden Hind*
  ran on,
Till the blast died down to a whispering breeze and a
  clean sun rose and shone;

And the albatross came wheeling to stare at their
  ribboned sail
As he dropped from the calm of the upper sky in the
  wake of the dying gale.

They rode alone in a lonely sea,—it was months
  before they knew
They would meet no more with their sister ships at
  the tryst in far Peru,

For the great untraversed ocean had claimed its first-
fruit prey,
And never a sign from the *Marygold* shall be till the
judgment day ;

But Wynter ran with the warning wind back into the
sheltered strait,
And there three weeks he had lingered on, for the
storm would not abate ;

Till at last with a waning hope or will, grown weary of
fight and foam,
He turned his back on the venture and set swift sail
for home.

So the might of the waves was broken, and the might
of the sun shone forth,
And eastward stretched a broad sea-way, but the land
lay west and north ;

Till then they had deemed that the austral earth with
a long unbroken shore
Ran on to the Pole Antarctic, for such was the old
sea-lore ;

But here were the sperm whales spouting for joy that
    the storm was done,
And the ice-floes sailing round them and the waves
    blue under the sun.

The sick men crept from their reeking bunks, and
    climbed to the decks again,
To see where the sister oceans met to the south of
    the gloomy main ;

And they hailed that storm for the wind of God,
    for the might of its blast had borne
The *Hind* on her path of glory a sea-league past the
    Horn.

They steered for the shadowy land they saw low
    under the northern sky,
To an isle unveiled by the lifting cloud, and they
    found good haven nigh :

They laughed and sang as they scaled the cliffs, and
    the New World rang with mirth,
And they stretched glad arms to heaven on the
    southermost earth on earth.

Thenceforth since proved by every test their stubborn
 faith prevailed,

Since earth and sky and ocean had spent their might
 and failed,

The Hand that binds the hurricane and holds the
 winds in fee

Made fair and smooth the untried ways across the
 promised sea.

III

Beyond the gloom of ice-scarred cliffs that bound
 that austral land

The coast trends north two thousand miles through
 plains of yellow sand.

But they saw dark-shadowing far inland the sudden
 Andes rise

With bleak and barren flanks that turn towards the
 sunset skies ;

For bounteous earth looks eastward there, and from
 her snow-capped crests

Great rivers flow to meet the dawn among her fruitful
 breasts.

But rarely some lone mountain tarn spills westward
    down the chain
A stream that feeds its borderlands of garden in the
    plain ;

So the ports where ships may enter are few and far
    between,
Where some such silver thread winds down to make
    the desert green.

They watched the snows of Andes slide past beneath
    the moon,
And felt the summer's breath once more blow down
    the mellow noon ;

The eager zest of life came back, they drank a glorious
 .   air,
Forgot the toil of weary months and winter's long
    despair.

IV

It was a fair November eve in Valparaiso Bay,
Where all aboard made taut for sea the treasure-
    galleon lay.

The crew were lounging o'er her sides to watch the
   setting sun,
And sweetly fell the end of day to men whose work
   was done.

A lazy mist hung o'er the stream and veiled the hills
   in blue,
And up the lime-washed belfry tower the rose of
   evening grew.

The ripple from the river ran a sheet of quivered
   flame,
And softly on the dropping breeze the bell's low
   tinkle came;

When round the distant headland a dark sail hove
   in sight,
A gallant bark stood up the bay, and swiftly fell the
   night.

An hour more and the last red glow on ocean's
   margin waned,
And through the pale star-clusters the queen moon
   rose and reigned.

The Spaniards broached a cask of wine, the crew
    stood by to greet
The ship come in from Panama with tidings from
    the fleet.

A boat has left the stranger craft, they hailed, and
    one replied,
And a score of sturdy Devon lads have swarmed the
    galleon's side ;

A sudden rush has cleared the decks, and up swarmed
    twenty more,
And the galleon's crew are overboard and striking out
    for shore ;

But her pilot hailed them friends, not foes, a Greek
    long years impressed,
An eager guide to steer the *Hind* along the unknown
    west.

Oh never draught of wine hath seemed so sweet to
    parching mouth
As that first cup they pledged on board the *Captain
    of the South !*

A panic seized the little port, the townsfolk fled
    inland,
And left their stores of Chili wine and all good things
    to hand.

So three days more Drake lingered here and stocked
    the ship afresh,
They had lived too long on melted snow and the
    bitter penguin flesh;

And the scurvy-stricken wretches laughed out for very
    mirth
As they culled the fruits they craved for and blessed
    the mother earth.

Then wind and current bore them north along the
    yellow main,
And the sound of fife and hautboy was heard on
    board again;

For keen as lads let loose from school, with reckless
    jest and boast
They raided every bight and bay that frets the silver
    coast.

And ere they left Arica's quays with all her ingots
    stored,
There was half-a-million ducats' worth of silver bars
    on board.

In splendid scorn of circumstance, with desperate odds
    to face,
They sailed those first intruders of our adventurous
    race ;

To-day a wiser, wearier world will brand them
    buccaneers ;
They did not doubt their cause was just in those
    distracted years.

In a little while all England's isle, like them, shall gird
    for fray.
The first who battle with the strong must use what
    arms they may.

But still no tidings came to hand of Wynter and his
    crew,
So they bore away for Lima and the spoils of rich
    Peru.

For every bark they had overhauled confirmed their
    pilot's tale,
That the richest prize in all those seas lay there and
    due to sail.

So they left the *Captain of the South* without a crew
    to drift,
Henceforth the *Hind* must sail alone, for the race is to
    the swift :

And fleeter than the tidings ran from shores their
    advent scared,
They sailed beyond their ill-renown and found men
    unprepared.

So they lay hove-to a sea-league off, and then with
    never a light
Ran up Callao di Lima in the dead of a murky night.

But the giant *Cacafuego* had sailed ten days before,
Deep laden to the water-line with all Potosi's ore ;

And while they ransacked empty hulls a wild alarum
broke
From clamouring bells and signal-guns, and startled
Lima woke;

Red torches flitted through the gloom, men mustered
on the quay,
And Drake must cut his cable-tow and hurry out to
sea.

But the light night breeze died down with dawn, and
there the rovers lay
With flapping sails struck motionless a short sea-league
away;

While rumour rode with panic spur, their one ship
grew to ten,
And the Viceroy of Peru marched down with twice
a thousand men.

He has manned and armed four galleons, with the
charge to take or burn
The dragon in his devil-ship, or nevermore return.

But still across a cloudless sky the slow sun climbed
　　and crept,
While like a sheet of milky glass the breathless ocean
　　slept ;

And morn and morrow's morning dawned, and still
　　like a drowsy spell
On land and water, friend and foe, the trance of
　　nature fell.

And now the watchers on the *Hind* beheld from those
　　clear shores
Two galleys move like living things on hundred-footed
　　oars ;

They heard their pulsing measured thud far off across
　　the calm
As they cleared their deck for action and sang the
　　battle psalm.

The general's cold blue eye surveyed the narrowing
　　space between,
" Now, lads," cried he, " to play the man, for God and
　　for the Queen ! "

But ere the answering cheer died down a dark flaw
    crimped the seas,
The ripple rattled on the stem, they sniffed the coming
    breeze :

The white sails filled, the good ship heeled, the merry
    land-wind blew,
And as a scared swan skims the lake she shook her
    wings and flew.

And now to crowd all canvas on and dog the *Spitfire's*
    wake,
There sails no craft of Panama shall show clean heels
    to Drake.

They tracked her north from port to port, they never
    lost the trace,
Eight hundred weary miles of sea, and yet she baffled
    chase.

She had lingered in Truxillo to load more treasure
    still,
She had watered at Paita, she had touched at
    Guayaquil.

It was hard on the Line on the first of March when
the morning broke at last,
They were 'ware of her square-rig far away, and they
knew that they held her fast.

So they shortened sail in the *Golden Hind* to wait till
the end of day,
And they trailed great casks and breakers at her stern
to check the way.

The sun was dropping down the west as they cut her
fetters free,
And like a greyhound slipped from leash she bounded
through the sea :

They hauled the chase as twilight fell—one flight of
arrows flew,
One broadside brought the mainyard down, and the
giant ship hove to.

Night strode across the heaving deep, night and the
unknown foe,
And the richest prize that ever sailed has struck
without a blow.

K

Her captain sits at meat with Drake, a sore unwilling
    guest,
And prize and captor side by side have set their
    courses west.

Far off in ocean's solitude, secure from all pursuit,
They overhauled the priceless freight and they found
    an empire's loot :

There were thirteen chests of minted coin, there were
    pearls and gems untold,
And all the ballast under decks was silver bars and
    gold.

The admiral of the treasure fleets at Nombre waits in
    vain,
For not one ounce of all that gold shall find its way
    to Spain.

The cruisers sent from Lima long since had cried
    despair,
The Dragon came they knew not whence, and was
    gone they knew not where.

So all the coast rose up in arms, and, as the panic
    grew,

The great ship came to Panama, a long month
    overdue ;

They had met, they said, with a corsair, whose like
    there was none on earth,

For the men at arms who served him were of England's
    gentlest birth ;

There was never a crew so ordered, so quick to the
    captain's call,

He lived like a prince in his state on board, and his
    will was a law for all.

They had brought a letter signed and sealed with a
    haughty word from Drake,

And the king's vice-regent gnashed his teeth as he
    read for anger's sake ;

" There be English seamen here," he wrote, "of my
    own old fellowship,

Whose limbs are chained to your galley bench, and
    red from the driver's whip,

" Henceforth I bid you give good heed that they
        come to no more harm,
Or I'll hang me a thousand Spaniards at the *Golden
        Hind's* yard-arm."

So frigates with despatches sailed post haste from
        Venta Cruz,
And soon Madrid and Lisbon rang with this disastrous
        news ;

Then Sarmiento put to sea to block Magellan's Strait,
And Philip's envoy found the Queen no novice in
        debate ;

Once more El Draque had dared transgress the sea's
        forbidden bar,
Had set the bulls of Rome at naught, perplexing
        peace with war ;

His liege of Spain would learn forthwith whose flag
        these corsairs fly !—
Not Cecil, but the Queen herself, returned the proud
        reply ;

"For proven wrong waits due redress ; but ill-timed
  comes your plea

When hireling bravos land and league with Desmond's
  Irishry :

"When all the claims myself have urged for wrongs
  to be redressed,

Still wait my kinsman's courtesy to be answered —
  for the rest,

"I have yet to learn what papal bulls run west of
  Finisterre

To bar my people's birthright in ocean, earth, and
  air !"

And thus the war of words ran high with claim and
  counterclaim,

And weeks and months rolled on for years—but of
  Drake no tidings came.

v

Three thousand miles to the frozen north on a track
  untried of man,

They had sought for the fabled outlet of the Straits
  of Anian ;

As many a stout heart yet shall sail in the years that
 are to be,
On the phantom quest of the drift north-west, through
 the heart of the iceberg sea.

But ever they beat in the teeth of storms, half blind
 with the threshing hail,
While the spray froze fast on gear and mast and
 starched their fretting sail ;

They came to the edge of a mountain world, where
 clouds hung heavy and low
On the gloom of the great fir forests, black under the
 crowning snow :

The sparkle died from the merry sea, and the fogs lay
 dank and thick
On the wan unfriendly waters, and half of his men
 fell sick.

But the trend of the land lay westward still, and icier
 struck the blast,   .
The work of three grew a toil for six, and they gave up
 hope at last.

So the *Hind* ran south with the wind in her wake till
    they chanced on a kindlier land,
And they set up forge and workshop, and they beached
    her on the strand.

The gentle tribes of the Indian folk came down to
    their camp unscared,
On a shore that the Old World's lust for gold or
    hunger of earth had spared :

They hailed them welcome, they brought them gifts, in
    wonder and love and awe,
And bowed at the feet of the great white gods who
    were come to give them law ;

They brought the wand of their chief of chiefs to set
    in the general's hand,
And with mystic rights proclaimed him the lord of
    the Indian's land.

So the English went to their upland towns, for the
    fringe of the hills was near,
Looked over the boundless pasture world and the
    untold herds of deer ;

The dust of that earth was agleam with gold, the
    skirt of the slopes was rare
With the tender growth of a northern clime, and
    spring was quick in the air.

There was many a lad was tempted then — begged
    hard to be left behind,
For they said, "We have wandered two full years at
    the chance of the fickle wind.

"So long we roam, and it's far to home, and weary of
    fight are we,"
But the captain frowned in silence as he led them
    down to the sea.

He piled a cairn on the cliffs' high crest with a graven
    plate thereon,
And Her Grace's name writ large to mark when her
    latest realm was won ;

He called that land New Albion, with a tender thought
    for home,
As they bade farewell to the gleaming rocks that
    rose through the whiter foam ;

The wild folk watched with wondering eyes, the
women crooned low wails,
For the fair white gods went seaward and the *Hind*
shook out her sails.

But the sea-queen's brood shall come once more to
that shore where the white cliffs are,
When the sons of their children's children have
followed the evening star;

Their bounds shall be either ocean, for the same
divine unrest
Shall drive their teeming millions to seek new fortunes
west;

And a great sea-city havened here shall leap to sudden
fame,
Re-echoing in an alien speech the great sea-captain's
name.

He laid his course by the Spaniard's chart, "For we'll
trust to the open sea,
And it's Westward Ho till the home-wind blows, as it
was from the start," said he.

"We are half-way round the world, my lads, and it's
    half-way round once more,
Till we've ploughed a track on the ocean's back that
    never was ploughed before. "

So they dropped to the edge of the North-East Trade,
    and they ran west sixty days,
With never a sight of shore or sail in the infinite
    ocean ways ;

And the mariner's boy through the long night-watch
    would brood on his heart's desire,
While the strange stars played with the dancing yards
    and the wake ran blue with fire ;

For the craving came that the wanderer knows for the
    lilt of his own folk's speech;
For the damp moss scents in the ancient grass and
    the shade of elm and beech,

For the rook's loud call in the twilight fall and the
    thin blue smoke that weaves,
The veil of mist on the red farm roof and the gold of
    the autumn leaves.

But weary wide were those seas untried, and little avail
to sigh
For the home stars in their places and the old
familiar sky.

Light lie the snows on byre and thatch, and windless
fall the rain,
Deal gently with them, summer sun, till we get back
again !

And at last they came to a mid-sea isle, and a cluster
of isles beyond
Swam up through the white mirage of dawn as if by a
fairy's wand ;

Up rose the sun, the long low swell slid landward
flushed with day,
And the golden message climbed the brows of an
upland far away ;

The flighting sea-birds overhead went clanging through
the sky,
But the ripple showed the white reef's edge, and they
dared not venture nigh.

So they left the clustering isles to dream through their
    drowsy moons and noons,
Safe walled in the coral girdles that glass their still
    lagoons ;

And they bore away for the Line once more till a
    fairway broadened free,
Where the perfume-laden breezes blow through the
    blue Molucca sea.

The bloom of the clove was harvested as they lingered
    to explore
The garden ways of the ocean realms of Ternate and
    Tidore ;

And they beached the *Hind* in a lonely isle where
    foot never yet, maybe,
Had stirred the sand of the shell-strewn strand since
    the isles came up from the sea.

All over its hills gigantic, weird, the silent forest grew,
With tapered stems to the tented roof that never a
    sun looked through ,

And even at midmost noon was gloom in the branchless
colonnade,

Where the bats and the flying foxes were lords of the
twilight shade,

Where great land-crabs in the twisting roots stared
out of their towering eyes,

And night was quick with the shifting light of the
myriad phosphor flies.

So there they abode for a month intrenched with the
bullion stacked on shore,

Till trimmed and taut for her long run home, she slid
to the deep once more.

Then west and south through the infinite isles, through
treacherous reefs that hide,

Where the dead volcanoes cumber the drift of the
parcelled tide ;

They were bound for the Sunda Channel, for the
chart gave free-way there,

They were two days out from Celebes, and the topsail
wind blew fair ;

There was never a sign on the false sea's face as she
 struck with a grinding shock,
As the keel ploughed through and the ship held fast
 in the crust of a sunken rock ;—

Oh many a time these two years back they had fought
 with the ague breath
That chills the heart of the bravest man when he looks
 in the face of death ;

But not in their mad race past the Horn, nor the jaws
 of the fearsome strait,
Not yet at the hand of God or man had they stood so
 near their fate.

And then, as ever in direst need, they bent the
 stubborn knee,
And said the brief and earnest prayer to the God who
 made the sea.

It was all deep water round the *Hind*, and the warps
 could find no stay,
And fast at the chance of a freshening breeze and
 a rising swell they lay ;

So they rolled the great guns overboard, and the
    spoils of rich Peru,
The shimmering ingots one by one went diving down
    the blue.

No craven panic blanched their cheeks though the
    good ship never stirred,
The ocean drill was perfect now,—one voice alone
    demurred:

What ailed you, Master Fletcher, there, brave heart in
    all beside,
To prate about the hand of God, and the death that
    Doughty died?

The little captain turned in wrath and flung him on
    the deck,
Set both his ankles in the stocks, and a posy round
    his neck,

"Lo here sits Parson Fletcher, the falsest knave
    alive!"
"For till her timbers part," said he, "I'll have no
    croaker thrive."

And so the weary day went down, and up the full
    moon sailed,
The broken waters tinkled by, and nought their toil
    availed ;

But tired and spent and sick at heart they watched
    the watches through :
"We are in the hand of God," said he ; "we have
    done what men may do."

And lo, the hand was stretched to save ;—as it drew
    towards the day
The breeze that held her broadside up grew slacker,
    died away ;

She heeled towards the deep once more, and so with
    never a strain,
By the mercy of God, as the morning broke, slid back
    to her own again.

Now, drawers, bring the Alicant of which we robbed
    the Don !
Go loose the parson from the stocks, and get his
    surplice on !

The leadsmen to the chains again, for Drake's
    triumphant star
Shall guide us through the Flores Sea and past the
    eastern bar !

So on by treacherous reef and shoal, by cape and
    channel and sound,
They groped their way through the island belt that
    girds the South Sea round ;

Behind them sank the shadowy shores, and they came
    on the ocean swell
Where the great tides heave untrammelled, and they
    knew that all was well.

VI

Now it fell one morn of the after-year there was stir
    in Plymouth fort,
And the guard turned out as the daylight broke to
    the Admiral of the Port,

For the watch on the Rame had sent him word of a
    warship hove in sight
That beat in the teeth of the keen north-east at fall
    of the autumn night ;

L

He searched the dawn with his keen sea eyes, for
    there sailed neither Dutch nor Don,
But veiled his tops to the English flag in the days of
    Admiral John.

And need was then for wary eyes, for the news was
    fresh to hand
Of galleons off the Irish coast with companies to land.

The white mist rose, a bare mile off she stood in over
    the bay,
And she bore her topsails proudly as one that had
    right of way :

" If ever the dead came back to life," it was old John
    Hawkins spake,
" I had sworn to that rig in a thousand ships for my
    kinsman's Frankie Drake."

And e'en as he spake the red cross flag shook out
    from her taper mast,
A thunder of guns broke right and left and the *Hind*
    was home at last !

Her beardless boys were seasoned men with necks
    set firm, and face
Tanned ruddy by the winds and suns that shape the
    sea-born race;

Her fluttering sails were patched and frayed, her
    bulwarks all a wreck,
The pitch ran through her open seams and stained
    her splintered deck;

Her painted prow was rusty brown with the crust of
    alien seas,
And half her ports were blind of the guns she had
    dropped in Celebes:

But every hand was up on deck or aloft on mast and
    spar
To cheer the dropping anchor down behind the
    harbour bar.

Oh golden spread the Edgcumbe woods and purpling
    leaned the down,
And lingering wreaths of yellow furze lit up the moor-
    land crown;

The world of home lay passing fair beyond the weary
　　seas,

As all the bells began to ring and the folk ran down
　　the quays.

From house to house, from street to street, the news
　　ran far and wide,

To Dart and Tamar, east and west, and up the
　　country-side.

The dead had all been duly mourned long since,
　　time out of mind,

There was only clasp of welcome hands and mirth on
　　board the *Hind ;*

VII

They have brought the *Hind* to Deptford town, they
　　have moored her by the quay, .

A bridge of plank athwart her waist,—she will go no
　　more to sea.

But pilgrims come from far and near and climb her
　　poop in pride,

And many a barge from Tower steps drops down
　　there on the tide ;

There's not a 'prentice in the Fleet but has felt a
    sailor born
The day he saw the famous ship that found and
    named the Horn ;

And scholars learned in the lore of great adventures
    past
Have turned conceits and epigrams to hang about her
    mast.

While Drake's tall lads, in silk and stuff, went swag-
    gering up and down,
With tales that turned the staidest heads, and ale ran
    free in town.

But now the windows all are wide, there are flags in
    every street,
For the Queen herself has come to-day to sit with
    Drake at meat.

The *Golden Hind's* great ordnance has fired the last
    salute,
The crew are marshalled on the poop with drum and
    fife and flute ;

The board is spread between the decks among the
    brazen guns,
For to-day the great Queen honours the bravest of her
    sons.

The captain of her guard was there in doublet slashed
    and pearled,
For Hatton's was the proud device they had carried
    round the world :

And subtle Master Walsingham with the long thin
    nervous hands,
Who knew the minds and manners of many folk and
    lands ;

And there was Martin Frobisher, the pilot of the Pole,
And Grenville, than whom England held no knightlier
    sailor soul.

There sat Sir Humphry Gilbert, the untimely lost,—
    not yet
In the vengeful night of ocean scorned his storm-
    tossed star had set ;

And Walter Raleigh new to court, and flushed with
fortune's smile,
The travelled Earl of Cumberland and Christopher
Carlile ;

With Sanderson, the man of maps, who drew the first
sea-card,
And Osborne, Mayor of London town, and the elders
of his ward,

Whose merchant fleets shall sail henceforth untrammelled east or west ;
And they spoke of deeds adventurous and all the
world's unrest.

So went she forth accompanied, that unforgotten day
She flung the Spaniard's challenge back, defiant ;—
these were they

Who first dared dream and dreaming dared—while all
was yet to do,
To roll the bounds of empire back beyond the bounds
they knew ;

To bind the winds their bondsmen, and hold the tide
     their slave,
And claim for island England dominion o'er the wave.

"Now hearken, lords and gentlemen, we have heard
     to-day," said she,
"Of the world beyond the sunset and the sea beyond
     the sea,

"But of piracies and plunderings, of trespass, raid,
     and wrong,—
Of this we learned from Philip's self, and the tale is
     passing long;

"And still my kinsman claims to know whose flag this
     bark hath flown
Which Master Drake hath dared maintain through
     seas he claims his own.

"Now therefore to such questionings let this my
     answer be,
Down, truant rover, down, and crave my pardon on
     your knee!"

Then he who fear had never known stood blanched
    before her seat,
Ungirt his sword and bowed and knelt to lay it at her
    feet.

And roundly there she rated him, and looked him up
    and down,
With eyes that knew a true man's worth, and smiled
    away their frown.

She bared his blade, she rose a queen, a queen to
    mar or make—
"My little pirate, rise," she cried, "and be Sir
    Francis Drake!"

MISCELLANEOUS

THE BALLAD OF RICHARD PEAKE

"A good ship I know, and a poor cabin; and the language
of a cannon : and therefore as my breeding has been rough,
scorning delicacy, so must my writings be, proceeding from
fingers fitter for the pike than the pen."—PEAKE'S *Narrative*.

THIS is the tale of Richard Peake,
　　Of Tavistock in Devon,
And the fight he fought in Xeres town,—
　　God rest his soul in Heaven !

I know each pool of Dart and Exe
　　Where trout or grayling hide,
I know the moors from sea to sea
　　And where the red-deer bide ;
I know a tall ship stem to stern
　　What sail to set or strike,
I know to point a culverin
　　And how to thrust a pike.

I know the star-way through the night
  And the bodings in the skies,
But many a man knows more than I
  That is not wondrous wise.
I cannot turn a silken phrase,
  Nor make a sonnet sing ;
Yet must I write my chronicle
  For my good Lord the King.
A western man and lowly born,
  And early sent to sea,—
So simple as my breeding was,
  Let this my record be.

Ye have heard my Lord of Essex
  How he sailed to Cadiz Bay,
With all King Charles' men of war
  Upon a Saturday.
We were sixteen sail of Holland,
  And a hundred of the line,
And I was pricked a volunteer
  Aboard the *Convertine.*
We had stormed the fort and castle
  From rising of the sun,

And long ere noon they landed
   And silenced every gun.
But I was no shore soldier,
   And so on board must bide
What time my Lord of Essex
   Marched up the country-side.

Now it fell on the Monday morning
   I took my leave ashore,
And walked up through the orange groves
   A mile might be, or more.
'Twas said the country-side was bare,
   The country-folk in flight,
A score of miles round Cadiz town,
   And not a don in sight ;—
When suddenly a cavalier
   His long sword at the thrust
Came spurring down the narrow way
   With a clatter through the dust.
His steed was checked, his grip was loosed,
   With a flap from my blue cloak ;
I clutched the rider by the heel,
   And caught the muffled stroke ;

I dragged him down upon his face
  And stripped him where he lay,
I took five silver pieces
  And a horse in that affray.
But while he begged his life in words
  That lisp on English ears,
There stole down through the orange groves
  His squad of musketeers :
And when my hands were bound behind,
  That knight to his disgrace
Took back the sword I stripped him of
  And slashed me in the face.

With seven guards on either hand
  And this brave knight before,
They brought me bound and bloody
  In through the city door ;
They gored my back with halberds
  And spat into my face.
The urchins called me heathen swine,
  God give them little grace !
They threw me into prison
  So bloodless and so weak,
It needed all their leeches

   To find me strength to speak ;
And vain it was my Captain sent
   To ransom Richard Peake.
I saw our frigates hoisting sail
   Upon the seventh day,
And through my dungeon window
   I watched them fade away.
Two Irish monks came every noon
   And wasted pious breath,
Abjuring me from heresy
   Since I must die the death ;
And when a week had passed they said
   It was the Governor's mind
That I should thence to Xeres town
   To the torture, they divined.

In Xeres Duke Medina lay
   With many a Count and Earl,
And gravely these good lords were met
   To try the English churl.
It was a pleasant sight to see
   Where they sat in double rows,
Such ruffles and such velvet cloaks

M

And slashen sleeves and hose !
The Duke sat at the table's head
   With the King's golden chain—
I mind no finer gentlemen
   Than gentlemen in Spain.

And there and then Medina's self
   Rebuked that craven knight
Who struck the prisoner in the face
   He dared not face in fight.

They plied me well with questions—
   What guns were in the fleet ?
What ship was mine ? what captain ?
   And I answered as was meet.

They asked how strong the fort was
   That watches Plymouth Sound,
And boastfully I lied my best
   As a Devon man was bound.

Quoth one, "Why spared ye Cadiz ?
   Your fleet put back to sea ! "
"Who loots," said I, "in palaces
   May let the almshouse be."

But all this while the soldiers round
   Made mirth each time I spoke,

And ugly words for English ears
    Went round the common folk :
Until some jest rang o'er the rest,
    And all those nobles smiled ;
Now God forbid that I should stand
    And hear my land reviled.

I said, "Your king keeps gallant troops
    To wear such bands and cuffs,
And they should hold in battle firm
    When the starch is in their ruffs.
Yet were I free to pick my choice
    From a score of oaken sticks,
I'd stand and play my quarterstaff—
    For life or death with six."
"Now, by the rood," Medina said,
    "A braggart though thou be,
I will not take thee at thy word,
    But fight thou shalt with three !"

And if I made so bold a face
    Be sure it was not pride,

But Richard Peake of Tavistock
   Had heard his land belied.
I deemed my death was long resolved,
   So basely would not die,
And three to one were heavy odds
   For a better man than I.
A halberd was my quarterstaff—
   They knocked the blade away,
The iron spike which shod the butt
   Stood me in stead that day.
I swung the halberd round my head
   And felt my might again,
And I took my stand for England
   Against the arch-foe Spain.

Then out stepped three hidalgos,
   Steel armoured cap-a-pie,
And lightly sprang into the lists
   With a mocking bow to me.
God save my Lord—though I must speak—
   It was a pretty fight.
Three long swords thrust and feinted
   In front, to left, to right ;

While round their heads the halberd swung
    And as they closed up near,
I snapped two blades, then shortened grip
    And used it as a spear;
I drove it at the third one's breast,
    And a horrid wound it made,
The iron butt went through his heart
    And out by the shoulder-blade.
And now befell a wondrous thing,—
    I needs must say again
Earth holds no finer gentlemen
    Than the gentlemen of Spain—

Those nobles rose and clapped their hands,
    The Duke was first to speak,
He bade no man on pain of death
    Lay hands on Richard Peake.
They gave me gold, a band and cuffs,
    This cloak I wear, the ring,
And sent me forth escorted well
    To see the Spanish King;
And in Madrid on Christmas Day
    I knelt before his sight,

Resolving all his questionings
  With what poor wit I might.
He would have had me bide in Spain
  To serve on shore or sea,
But I've a wife by Tavy side
  And she's got none but me.
Wherefore he pitied my estate
  And pardon free bestowed,
With a hundred pistoles in my scrip
  For charges on the road.
And so I bade Madrid farewell,
  And came without annoy
Through France to Bordeaux haven,
  And thence took ship to Foy.

Now while the Tamar winds to sea,
  And while the Tavy runs,
God bless my old west country,
  And God bless all her sons !
It's not in vain we've tracked the deer
  By dale and moor and fen,
And drunk the morning with our lips,
  And grown up brawny men.

It's not in vain we swam the Sound,
    And tugged the heavy oar,
And braced the nerve and trained the limbs
    That English mothers bore.
And therefore when the fight goes hard,
    And the many meet the few,
She'll still find hands to do the work
    That English lads must do.
So here I render thanks to God,
    Who brought me through the sea,
Across the desert, back again,
    My mother-land, to thee.

This was the tale of Richard Peake
    Of Tavistock in Devon,
And the fight he fought in Xeres town,—
    God rest his soul in Heaven!

HAWKWOOD

"WHO'LL ride with me," said rough Sir John,
　　"In quest of new adventure?
The Black Prince over seas has gone,
　　And cancelled our indenture.

"The Duke of Milan sends to France
　　Enlisting sturdy fighters,
And I've a mind to break a lance
　　Against the Saxon Reiters.

"The Pisan and the Florentine
　　Renew their ancient tussle,
And Guelph outbids the Ghibelline
　　For English blood and muscle.

" They say the world has softer skies
    Beyond the Alpine passes,
Where fiercer fires light up the eyes
    Of more bewitching lasses ;

" They say that there on summer hills
    The grapes grow sweet as honey,
And there the threadbare trooper fills
    His saddle-bags with money ;

" So Jock and Hal may sail for home,
    And swear their old loves sweeter,
But I will ride the road to Rome,
    And see the grave of Peter."

Sir John he crossed the mountain bar
    With a troop of fifty banners,—
He taught the Guelph the art of war,
    He taught the Ghibelline manners.

Fate prospered all he took in hand,
    The years were full of chances,
And all the laurels in the land
    Were wreathed for Hawkwood's lances.

There in an age that held the name
  Of free-lance in abhorrence,
He won an honest soldier's fame
  With the sword he drew for Florence.

So Arno's bank and Elsa's vale,
  And blue Carrara's quarries,
Have heard the clink of English mail
  What time he rode his forays.

And there he saw his eightieth year,
  And died a right good fellow,
And there her greatest Condottier
  Was frescoed by Uccello;

And still beside Our Lady's door,
  Who holds the lily-flower,
He rides on guard for evermore
  In the shade of Giotto's tower.

THE DUKE HAS FRIENDS

My answer is—fill up your glass!—With you, Sir
    John, the Port!
They may call him traitor if they dare, and hound
    him from the Court!

There's many a courtier I could name has had his
    fingers black
With dipping after dirty coin in some one else's sack.

But you and I may only know we've drawn for
    England's right,
Behind the greatest captain that ever rode to fight!

Have you forgotten Eckerslau when the balls were
    thick as rain,

And we thought the word would never come to take
    the field again :

When the battle hung in balance, and we waited for
    his sign :

Do you remember what you felt as he cantered down
    the line ?

His breast was all one blaze of stars, his wrists were
    ruffed with lace,

The wind blew back his scented hair and showed his
    splendid face ;

The bullets snarled like angry wasps, the cannon
    thundered loud,

As he drew his rein before our ranks, and raised his
    hat and bowed ;

"With your permission, gentlemen of the English
    cavalry,

Myself will lead you to the charge,—sound trumpet,
    charge !" said he.

And calm as in the hunting-field he wheeled his
chestnut round,
And all the line behind him leapt forward with a
bound.

Then when the fight was over, and Blenheim lost
and won,
And England's greatest day went down in triumph
with the sun,

I see him as he bowed once more in answer to our
cheers,
That splendid English gentleman, that prince of
cavaliers!

The town may talk its head off—I care not who they
tell,
The Duke! his health in bumpers, and the court
may go to Hell!

QUIBERON

Sir Edward Hawke the Admiral
    Had trapped the French in Brest,
When a gale that blew a hurricane
    Came driving from the west.

The cruising fleet bore up awhile
    To shelter in Torbay—
The wind went round and stealthily
    The Frenchmen slipped away.

So the quidnuncs of the coffee shops,
    The loafers of the Strand,
And the watermen from Tower stairs
    Had a merry job in hand.

They made a mimic man of straw,
 With hose and buckled shoe,
With frogged tail-coat and gold-laced hat,—
 An Admiral of the Blue.

They hauled him down to Westminster
 And fixed him on a pike,
And there they burned in effigy
 The Hawke that did not strike.

But while that mob in London town
 Proclaimed their panic spite,
Between the shoals and Croisic roads
 He had fought his great sea-fight;

Five days he chased them southwards
 And east before a gale,
Till 'twixt Bellisle and Quiberon
 They counted twenty sail.

That angry sea was thick with reefs,
 A lee-shore loomed behind,
But Hawke dashed in at headlong speed
 Close-reefed before the wind;

And in the gate of Quiberon,
    At noon the self-same day
That rabble burned his effigy,
    The Hawke had struck his prey.

Choiseul may sell his transports now
    To quench his troopers' thirst,
The fleet that menaced England
    Is shattered and dispersed ;

September rang with Minden's news,
    October won Quebec,
November's gales and Quiberon
    Achieved the final wreck.

And the quidnuncs of the coffee shops
    Felt very big and brave,
And swore once more that Englishmen
    Were born to rule the wave.

THE FIRST OF JUNE

That fight shall be remembered while sea-tides ebb
    and flow,
That fight that fell on the first of June a hundred
    years ago;

What time in the mid-Atlantic, far out of the ken of
    shore,
The flag of the double crosses was matched with the
    tricolor.

The fleets were even ship for ship, and man for man
    the crews,
And braver seaman never sailed than Villaret-Joyeuse.

N

When Howe broke through his battle line, the first to
  join the fray,
The *Vengeur* shook her top-sails out and raced to bar
  the way ;

The *Brunswick* steering for the gap was next to
  gallant Howe,
And driving on before the wind she struck her on the
  bow ;—

The forechains held her anchor fast, she swung and
  could not free,
So tethered in a deadly grip those two dropped off to
  lee.

Our English blew their ports away, the shock had
  jammed them to,
They rammed their guns with shot and chain and
  raked the *Vengeur* through.

While hand to hand on the upper deck the Frenchmen
  swarmed to board,
Redressed the balance of the fight with grape and
  pike and sword :

That long forenoon the battle raged they scarce knew
    how or where,
Who, shrouded in a sulphur mist, fought out their duel
    there.

Our figure-head was Brunswick's Duke, who died at
    Auerstadt,
Now it chanced a round shot carried off the Duke's
    three-cornered hat.

Brave Captain Harvey lay below with the wound of
    which he died,
But as the word passed round the decks he raised him
    on his side,

And, "God forbid King George's fleet or Admiral
    Howe should see
The gallant Duke uncover to Villaret," says he.

His strength was ebbing as he spoke, but smiling
    through the pain,
"I shall not need," he whispered, "to wear my own
    again,"

"Take my cocked hat and brush away the powder
    from the lace,
And send for Jack the carpenter to nail it in its place."

The bullets snarled and spattered thick where'er a
    face might show,
But Jack just said "Aye, aye, sir," and touched his
    hat to go.

They watched him crawl out on the boom, they lost
    him in the smoke,
And through a pause of battle roar they caught his
    hammer's stroke.

But when the breeze a moment's space blew all the
    forecastle clear
There rose from half a thousand throats a ringing
    English cheer:

For Jack was back at quarters begrimed and black and
    torn,—
"And the Duke does not uncover, lads, to any
    Frenchman born!"

You know the rest,—the long swell grew, the vessels
    strained and heeled
Till the grapple parted, and away the stricken *Vengeur*
    reeled ;

Her spars still swung, but rudderless she drifted o'er
    the seas,
And lost the mastless *Brunswick* to close with the
    Ramillies.

An hour more and waterlogged she rolled a helpless
    wreck,
But still she bore the tricolor above her bloody deck.

When seven ships had struck their flags and that great
    fight was done,
When the shrouding smoke drew up and off towards
    the setting sun,

They saw her sinking slowly down with all her dying
    brave,
And boats put out in eager haste to succour and to
    save.

Too late, alas, to rescue all—the sea winds took their
    cry,
The cool waves washed their fevered wounds and they
    died as heroes die.

All honour to the men who wore the tricolor cockade,
All honour to the *Vengeur* for the splendid fight she
    made !

And to our own brave sailor lads all honour then as
    now,
But when the first of June comes round and you drink
    to gallant Howe,

Remember Jack the carpenter who held his life in
    scorn,
If Brunswick should uncover to any Frenchman born.

AT STRATHFIELDSAY

THE Autumn sun went down on Strathfieldsay,—
An old man rode by shadowy lawn and dell,
The old horse turned and took the homeward way,
And sweetly evening's benediction fell.
Then—wreathing smoke and grove and gable-crest,
Melting together in the sunset skies,
Piled a fantastic fabric in the west,
And touched the chord of sleeping memories.
He saw it all;—there frowned the battled height,
Here flowed Aguéda livid in the glare,
Ciudad Rodrigo blazed into the night,
And cannon thundered through the misty air;—
Sounds of far voices, silent long ago,
Rose like faint echoes, and close by his side
Familiar forms seemed flitting to and fro,
While darkness gathered and the red glow died.

The old horse whinnied, and he bowed his head,

The twilight mellowed to its own again,—

"All *that* I lived through ! and they all are dead !

Grant us Thy peace, God merciful.   Amen !"

TENNYSON

In to the silent Abbey, to the heroes' burying-place,
Bear him and leave him lying, peer with the peers
   of his race !

With the men of debate and battle, the mighty of
   heart or of brain,
Warders of Empire's outposts, home with their own
   again :—

Fitting is their death-welcome—the masks of his
   great compeers
Wrapt in the trance of silence—fitter for him than
   tears.

Never a sigh escort him, he has lived the tale of his
    days,
His burial-wreath is the laurel, his dirge is a nation's
    praise.

Why do we call him hero? Why do we bury him
    here?
Why are all England's greatest gathered about his
    bier?

Wandering sons she hath many, erring and loved no
    less,
But this was the son of her heart, and his strength
    was his faithfulness.

Singer of England's saga, back to the misty prime,
Rolling a morning glamour over the night of time;

Singer of English gardens, poet of English springs,
Lover of earth's dear beauty, and all elemental things.

Never a girl in England, or in England over the sea,
But wakes to her life's first love-dream sweetlier-souled
    for thee.

Never a boy's young life-blood thirsts for the dawn
    of deeds,
But it throbs to a nobler impulse as he turns thy roll
    and reads.

That was his lofty level, all that is hard and high,
All that is purely purposed, theme of his minstrelsy :

Never for easy guerdon—the goodliest gift disgraced—
Flinging a tainted poison down to a morbid taste :

Never a doubt or shadow cast on a virgin soul,
But love in a pure white garment, and faith in an
    aureole ;

Lending the mute thought language, flame to the
    waning fire,
A voice for the dream of the simple, a song for the
    world's desire.

For his heart was the heart of a child, and of such
    since time began
Are those the Eternal uses to speak to the heart of
    man.

PUMWANI

Comrades mine of *Blanche* and *Swallow* scattered
    now a hundred ways,
Such a march we made together, once in torrid
    August days!

Up the mangrove creeks we laboured, where the
    crooked roots divide,
Clutching fast the shoaling mud-banks and encroach-
    ing on the tide;

Gaunt and hideous rose the baobabs with their bloated
    stems and bare,
And their gray arms stretching naked to the rank and
    steamy air;

There we slept beneath the mangoes on forsaken
 village sites,
And drank in the cool refreshment of the wind-swept
 tropic nights,

Till at last the word was forward! and a noiseless
 camp awoke,
And the line fell into order ere the blush of morning
 broke.

Faint our track wound through the clearings, with
 their rank grass shoulder high,
Right and left the dense black forest walling in a
 tropic sky ;

Where the gum-vine binds the branches and the
 fiercely fecund soil
Bars the way to human ingress, tightens tangles into
 coil.

The thorn palm took fantastic shapes and drooped a
 withered skirt,
The vultures rose into the blue to give the woods
 alert.

Each followed close on his fellow's steps in the single
    serpent file,—-

Like the gray baboons at the forest edge,—and the
    line reached half a mile.

The black marsh water splashed our knees, the ooze
    sucked down our boots,

The slimy mud-fish wriggled off and hid in the tangled
    roots.

And every man held back his breath of all three
    hundred men,

For the dropping shots gave warning we were near the
    robber den.

Then a bugle broke the stillness of that forest edged
    with eyes,

Then a wild uproar of drumming and a thunder to the
    skies ;

Tongues of flame and battle rattle, puffs of smoke
    along the green,

Silent pauses in the volleys, and the foe we fought
    unseen :

Yet our little line drew closer, creeping on by slow
 degrees,
While the rockets like winged dragons ploughed a fire
 track through the trees.

And the minutes passed like hours, and the burning
 sun beat down,
Till ere noon drank up the shadows we were in the
 rebel town.

Once again the heart beat lightly and a sense of
 triumph grew,
For the fort was well defended and great gaps were in
 our few.

Swiftly fell the tropic evening, and, while camp fires
 flickered red,
We drew softly off on one side and we gathered up
 our dead ;—

By a lantern's feeble flicker read the words with which
 we trust
This our brother to God's keeping, this his body to
 the dust.

Dug a trench for you to lie in, you whose home was
    on the wave,

You the white man with the dark men, your bedfellows
    in the grave,

White and black both dead for England, with the
    grass mats round your heads,—

And we turned and left them lying in their solitary
    beds.

So world over sleep the English, eyes of friends will
    never look

Through that gloom of Afric forest where we buried
    Stoker Cook.

Only gray baboons will chatter in the branches where
    you lie,

And the quick hyena scamper through the tangle
    silently ;

Yet such meed of due remembrance I would yield
    you as I may,

Since you gave your life for England—have her
    greatest more to say ?

Since last night we slept together, 'twixt the grasses
and the star,
And to-night you sleep for ever by the bitter chance
of war.

But the camp was quick with laughter, for the blood
was beating high,—
Laugh out, life is for the living, for the dead at most
a sigh.

And the men whose hearts are boys' hearts set the
lanterns in a ring,
And the battle dawn's reaction made the peace of
evening sing.

So the old sea-songs came rolling till the chorus
shook the trees,
And the tropic stars looked wondering at the men
from over seas.

Then the hand-shake and the silence, and brief sleep
for those who may.
Let to-morrow take its chances, we have lived our
lives to-day.

EAST AFRICA, 1893.

O

TO GERALD PORTAL

A BLOOD-RED sky, a milky sea ;
    And home almost in hail,
And you that walked the deck with me
    To watch that glory pale !

I think my eyes had never seen
    So grand an even sky,
As that which ushered Europe in,
    You only reached to die.

Was it there first I learned to know
    How much you were to me ?
Though neither spoke, for that red glow
    Had struck the silent key.

The torrid suns were far behind,
    The toil of dreary days,
The breaths of poison striking blind,
    The wild untrodden ways :

I had no doubts, I never thought
    Those kind and fearless eyes,
Those strong unfaltering hands, were wrought
    Of stuff that lightly dies.

O fierce dark land, unconquered still,
    Though doomed to our behest,
How long ere thou hast drunk thy fill
    Of the blood of England's best !

The ship glides on, and overhead
    The moonless night succeeds,—
Henceforth whenever skies are red
    I may think my own heart bleeds.

1894.

NOTES

SAN JUAN DE LUA

Though many had held it was God's work too, etc.
   Page 15.

The experiment of introducing African negroes into
the West India Islands was first suggested by the
excellent bishop Las Casas, who recommended the
purchase of prisoners for this object on the West
African coast, where barbarous *customs* devoted the
weaker races to human sacrifice or the orgies of
cannibalism, on the plea that their servitude would
save them from a horrible fate and enable them to be
made Christians. It is stated that while the slave-trade
gave these prisoners a material value, the *customs* of the
dominant races were suspended.

THE REPRISAL

The fierce black tribes of the Cimaroons. Page 69.

Cimaroons or Maroons : Sp. Cimarrones.
" Eighty years ago a number of African slaves had

been driven by the cruelty of their masters to take to the woods, and having found favour in the eyes of the Indian women, they had now grown into two great tribes, whose terrible mission it was to rob, and kill, and torture every Spaniard on whom they could lay their hands."—Corbett's *Drake*, p. 23.

THE WORLD ENCOMPASSED

And bared the sword his arm alone might wield in honour bound. Page 110.

The fact that Drake himself was the executioner of Thomas Doughty, taking thus the full responsibility on his own shoulders, is recorded in the correspondence of the Spanish envoy. Mendoza, who cross-examined Wynter on the whole episode, showed a suspicious interest in his fate.

They had sought for the fabled outlet of the Straits of Anian. Page 133.

The name given to the supposed northern passage between the two oceans, the existence of which was an article of faith with the old mariners.

Re-echoing in an alien speech the great sea-captain's name. Page 137.

It is believed that the city of San Francisco occupies the site where Drake set up the pillar and inscription,

recording that he had taken possession of " New Albion "
in the name of Queen Elizabeth.

*For Hatton's was the proud device they had carried
round the world.* Page 150.

A Golden Hind was the crest of Christopher Hatton,
the Captain of the Guard, who was one of the chief
promoters and shareholders in the venture. In chang-
ing the name of the *Pelican* to the *Golden Hind*, Drake
diplomatically identified with his enterprise one of the
reigning favourites at court.

THE FIRST OF JUNE

*The flag of the double crosses was matched with the
tricolor.* Page 177.

The French fleet which took part in this memorable
battle was the first which used the tricolor flag.

The third cross was only added to the Union Jack in
1801. The original flag was the red cross of St. George,
to which St. Andrew's cross was added by James I.

THE END

Printed by R. & R. CLARK, LIMITED, *Edinburgh.*